ELIZABETH HOPKINSON is an award-winning author from Bradford, West Yorkshire, best known for the *Asexual Fairy Tales* series and podcast, and the *Angelio* series of YA historical fantasy novels.

She is a Voyager member of the Community of Aidan & Hilda, a dispersed, ecumenical body drawing inspiration from the lives of the Celtic saints.

Elizabeth is also an asexual rights activist, who appeared on Stonewall's first Ace/Aro panel, and a member of the Open Table Network, a growing network of Christian communities that affirm and welcome LGBTQIA+ people and allies.

Find out more about Elizabeth at: elizabethhopkinson.uk

ANNA HOPKINSON is a 25 year-old book and children's book illustrator from Bradford, UK. She is best known for illustrating the *Asexual Fairy Tales* series.

To see more of her work, visit her website: annahopkinsonart.com

Also By Elizabeth Hopkinson

Asexual Fairy Tales
Asexual Myths and Tales
More Asexual Fairy Tales

Praise for Elizabeth Hopkinson

"We always have a huge demand for asexual themed books, but sadly there's just not that many good titles around at the moment. Both *Asexual Myths & Tales* and *Asexual Fairy Tales* by Elizabeth Hopkinson sell really well for us and we've had amazing feedback from our customers for both of them. We literally can't wait to read the latest Ace stories from Elizabeth."

— Jason Guy, Director of Gay Pride Shop, Manchester

"We are SO excited to hear of a new collection of Asexual Tales from Elizabeth - the first two have been a huge success for the bookshop. When there is still so little asexual representation in print it's really thrilling as booksellers to be able to offer brilliantly written and produced titles offering just that to our readers - we will always welcome more!"

— Mairi (she/her), Lighthouse - Edinburgh's Radical Bookshop

"These Asexual Fairy Tales sound like old folk tales, perfect for reading out loud. More than just a retelling or adaptation, Elizabeth has succeeded in creating something new without losing that old-world storyteller feel."

— Jaylee James, editor of *Circuits and Slippers*

"Fairy tales are a part of every child's life. As we grow up, we learn mythology, history, and legends. Yet, for asexuals, the representation has always been rare to non-existent. What Elizabeth Hopkinson has done is brought aces to the forefront in these pieces of writing. It's an incredible and necessary thing! Everyone wants to see a character that is like themselves in what they read or watch, even when it comes to fairy tales. So what Elizabeth is doing here is greatly appreciated, and we wish her the very best!"

— Kelsey Lee, Social Media Director of AVEN

Legends from Lindisfarne

Diverse and Inclusive Saints

Elizabeth Hopkinson

Illustrated by Anna Hopkinson

SilverWood

Published in 2024 by SilverWood Books

SilverWood Books Ltd
14 Small Street, Bristol, BS1 1DE, United Kingdom
www.silverwoodbooks.co.uk

ISBN 978-1-80042-292-6 (paperback)

British Library Cataloguing in Publication Data
A CIP catalogue record for this book is available from the British Library

Page design and typesetting by SilverWood Books

*For all my siblings in
the Community of Aidan & Hilda*

Contents

Foreword

by Sister Thenue Rodden
Deputy Guardian, Community of Aidan & Hilda

It is my great pleasure to introduce this remarkable book by Elizabeth, a talented writer with a profound heart for the LGBT+ community and those on the fringes of society. Identifying as asexual, and as someone comfortable with liminality, Elizabeth has dedicated herself to unearthing fragments of long forgotten tales from the margins, and has woven them together into cohesive and beautiful narratives.

Through her collection of short stories, Elizabeth has crafted deeply moving and authentic narratives, where her earthy prose doesn't shy away from difficult realities, such as in her telling of Saint Thenue's story, approaching even the harshest truths, like rape, with a sensitivity and unflinching honesty that is both raw and profoundly human.

I read Elizabeth's manuscript over several days with the comforting ritual of a fresh cup of coffee and the eager anticipation of discovering a new favourite story. With every turn of the page, her writing consistently drew me in, assuring me that I was about to be fully engaged in a narrative that would linger with me for the rest of the day, if not much longer. The anticipation of the next story became a cherished part of my day, knowing each one would offer something uniquely profound and memorable.

There is so much depth to these stories. I love how cleverly and beautifully Elizabeth has woven Saint Morwenna's story into that of Robert Hawker, their entwined narrative enriching the overall tale. The story of Marinos, a saint who was wrongfully accused and vindicated only after death, moved me deeply and humbled me too, remembering the last time I was falsely accused and didn't handle it quite so graciously! In the tale of Muirgen the Mermaid Saint, Elizabeth invites us to find solace and strength in our own 'otherness', reminding us that feeling too strange, too old, or too different to belong is a shared human experience.

Through these stories, Elizabeth offers inspiration and connection, not only to the marginalised who feel they are standing on the threshold of society and identity, but to everyone, as we all universally experience moments of doubt and liminality. Her tales resonate with universal narratives of hope, inspiration and connection.

Prepare to be engaged, moved, and inspired. Elizabeth's book is a treasure, and I am honoured to present it to you.

From the Author

When Sister Thenue first suggested this project to me – a book similar to my *Asexual Fairy Tales* series, but retelling stories of the Celtic saints – I decided fairly quickly that I wanted it to highlight diversity and inclusion, something close to both our hearts.

In recent decades, many saints have been adopted by marginalised groups, including the LGBTQIA+ and disabled communities. So, we have in this book a mermaid saint, a trans monk, a nonuplet warrior, a socially anxious saint, and a Madonna who protects same-sex couples, to name but a few. Most of these saints are among those celebrated by the Community of Aidan & Hilda, with a few later inheritors of the 'Celtic' tradition. Although they are largely centred on the 'Celtic lands' (Ireland, Wales, Brittany, etc), they also embrace Lebanon, India, North America and Brazil.

Most books of saints' lives are aimed at Christian believers, and focused on the spiritual lessons to be learned from their life and/or devotion to the saint. Or they are focused on the legendary aspects of saints' lives, as explored by folklorists, storytellers, etc. I wanted my book to do both. My retellings come from a place of Christian faith, and draw on the wider Celtic spirituality and symbolism that will be familiar to neopagans. I hope people of all faiths and none can find common ground here.

Elizabeth Hopkinson,
July 2024

Thenue:

The Survivor

Thenue:

The Survivor

In the Kingdom of the Gododdin, on the banks of the Firth of Forth, there lived a Celtic princess named Thenue.

Fierce in battle were the Gododdin, celebrated in verse as far as Gwynedd, to whose people they were tied by kinship. Their ancient capital on the rock of Traprain Law had stood since Roman times, filled with shining silver and intricate carvings.

But Thenue was no warrior. She was only thirteen. Still, she was the daughter of a great chieftain - King Loth of Lothian, no less - and had her role to play. A royal daughter must make a strategic match, and so become a peace weaver between tribes that could so easily come to war otherwise.

So it was that Owain ap Urien came to Traprain Law, seeking Thenue's hand. A man of great fame, he was said to be a warrior of Arthur himself, and the hero of numerous tales.

Be that as it may, his suit was unsuccessful. Negotiations broke down. Owain would return to Gwynedd without Thenue as a bride.

Now, some say he had been captivated by Thenue's beauty. Or maybe the refusal was too great a humiliation for one such as he. However it was, that night a strange woman came to Thenue's chamber.

She was taller and more angular than most women, and walked with a heavy-footed stride. And when her head shawl slipped a little, Thenue was sure she had a hairy chin.

"It's a chilly night." The woman's voice was surprisingly deep. "Won't you keep me warm for a while?"

And before Thenue knew what was happening, the stranger had her flat on her back against the bed of wolf skins, her skirts ruched up.

"What are you doing?" Thenue gasped.

"Just a little something to keep us warm." By now, the stranger's skirts were hitched up also. Thenue's eyes widened at what she saw between the other's legs.

"Don't only males have...one of those?" She thought of her father's hunting hounds and the tough hill ponies of Traprain Law.

"Oh, no. This is how all grown women look. When you are grown, you will have one, too. Now, lie still and don't cry out."

Poor Thenue was so young, she was easily overpowered. If she tried to protest, the stranger assured her this was a natural rite of passage between women.

"And it must never be spoken of," said the stranger. "At risk of offending the Great Mother herself."

By the time Thenue was left alone, she was frightened, shamed, confused, pained.

Thus did Owain ap Urien take his revenge upon the Gododdin. He returned to Gwynedd and thought no more about it.

But Thenue was unable to forget, nor to keep the secret for very long. A few months later, her very pregnant belly was evident to all.

King Loth was outraged. Not with Owain (for Thenue was too afraid to name him) but with his own daughter for bringing shame upon his house and name. Such a crime was punishable by death.

Thenue – this confused and frightened child – was strapped to a chariot on the very brink of Traprain Law. There, where the Maiden Stone breaks away from the Mother Rock, the chasm descends 725 feet. Here, young brides squeeze between rock and stone, hoping to be blessed with many children.

But Thenue was neither maiden nor bride. And the child in her belly apparently brought blessing to no one.

Weighed down by the iron chariot, she was pushed off the rock, to her death.

Only Thenue did not die; nor did her unborn child.

Of course, she was not unharmed by the fall. The crippling injuries she sustained would be with her for life. But when King Loth saw that she had neither died nor miscarried, he was wroth.

"Witchcraft! Only a witch could fall from such a height and live."

And Thenue, who had suffered pain upon outrage, terror upon shame, was thrown into a coracle and set adrift in the Firth of Forth, at a place called the Mouth of Stench. She had not so much as an oar to steer her. If she survived her injuries from the fall, she would surely die of dehydration or exposure, whichever got her first.

The sky was grey and Thenue drifted alone. The world, it seemed, had abandoned her. She was betrayed, accused, punished by the very people who were meant to care for her. Surely, she deserved this. There was no other explanation. She had offended the Great Mother, and this was to be her end.

As the moon rose, something silver glinted in the water. A great shoal of fish was swimming alongside the coracle, nudging it gently to shore. And in the face of the moon, she thought she saw a woman, young and pregnant as Thenue herself. Her rounded belly glowed with the light of the sun and stars.

"Who are you?" Thenue's lips didn't move, and yet she spoke.

"I am the Great Mother of the Great Son." The woman's voice rippled through Thenue's head. "Like you, I was accused, yet I was innocent of blame. My son was sent from God. Take comfort from me, Thenue. You have been done a great wrong. None of this is your fault."

By now, her pains were great, yet Thenue took comfort from the words of the God-bearer. The fish nudged her coracle until it beached on the Isle of May. There, Thenue could crawl ashore to be discovered by the islanders, weak and thirsty, but alive.

They took her to Culross, where a missionary monk called Serf had a monastery – a kind of holy village, where the huts of the monks were surrounded by farmland and those who worked it. Serf and his monks were skilled in healing, and tended Thenue's wounds. In those days, not all monks were men, nor were all unmarried. There were plenty in the community who were knowledgeable in midwifery, when the time came.

"You are welcome here," Serf said to Thenue, when she was well enough to understand. "You have nothing to fear in this place. The past is past."

Slowly, in the care of this kind but unusual family, Thenue began to heal. And if she never walked straight again, there was a new lightness in her soul. When she held her newborn son in her arms for the first time – his damp little head against her breast – she felt a wave of love, glittering as a shoal of fish.

"I shall call him Kentigern," she said. "Great Chieftain. It is his birthright."

And so she did. But Serf later gave him a nickname that stuck just as well. He called the lad Mungo. The Dear One. This child born out of wedlock, the product of rape. With that name, all sense of shame was removed.

It was said that, later in life, Thenue became the abbess of her own holy village, taking in women who had suffered violence, and caring for them. They say that in Glasgow where she was buried, a holy well sprang up, where women would come for healing. And when twenty-nine Glasgow girls and women died in a collapsed weaving shed, it was Thenue's image that became their memorial. A mural was painted in their memory, commissioned by the housing society that bears Thenue's name. They call her Protector of the Abused.

Thenue stands out among saints, not for performing great miracles, but as a recipient of divine provision. The unseen hand cushioned her fall and guided her to a place of safety. Here, she was shown what love really is, and the healing she received enabled her to live with her wounds and to care for others, bringing hope to their darkness.

Muirgen:

The Mermaid Saint

Muirgen:

The Mermaid Saint

I f you should ever think yourself too strange, too odd, too different to belong, take heart from the story of Muirgen. For three hundred years, she swam beneath the waves, with only a dog-otter for company. She was a creature of another age. When last she walked with feet, the Tuatha Dé Danann were yet abroad in Ireland. Now, Ireland was become a land of saints and scholars. And Beoan, son of Innle, caught Muirgen in his net.

It happened this way. Comgall, the abbot of Bangor, had dispatched Beoan, the abbot of Loughbrickland, on a mission to Pope Gregory in Rome. As Beoan's curragh set sail into the Irish Sea, the crew heard a sound from the waters like the singing of angels.

Beoan leaned out into the wind. "Who is that, singing?"

Imagine his surprise when a strange creature surfaced. From the waist upwards, a woman; from the waist downwards, a salmon.

"It is I, Liban," said the creature.

The sailors gaped, their hands idle. Liban means 'mermaid'. They had all heard of mermaids, but never seen one in the flesh.

Beoan was equally fascinated. He thought of the books of learning at the abbey: ancient bestiaries filled with unusual beasts. Had he found a curiosity? Or was this Liban a person with a soul, just like him?

"Where do you come from?"

"Lough Neagh'" came the surprising answer. The enormous lough was some way inland. "I am the daughter of Eochaid, son of Mairid."

"But that's..." Beoan blinked. "Eochaid lived hundreds of years ago." If he lived at all, Beoan thought. Was not Eochaid one of the faery race? The Tuatha Dé Danann. Yet here was a mermaid, as real as any

23

man, claiming to be Eochaid's daughter. "Will you tell me your story?" The mermaid was fast dropping behind the stern of the boat, yet he had to know more. Another thought struck him. "Would you come to my monastery and be baptised?" Imagine baptising one of the Tuatha Dé Danann! Those Irish who still held to the old gods would think differently if they saw a creature from myth accept the Way of Jesus.

Liban shrugged one silvery shoulder. "If you're serious, then meet me up the coast at Larne, one year from now. I'll tell you everything. But don't play me false, or woe betide!"

"And what will you give me if I keep the tryst?" Beoan called.

But Liban had vanished into the waves.

Could she trust the monk? Liban asked the question over and again as the year wore on. In her day, there had been no monks in Ireland. Now she often heard their bells and the chanting of psalms drifting over the waves. They liked to live in sea caves and on islands, testing the limits of body and mind, much as the druids had before them. Perhaps they had something in common with her, caught between sea and land? Perhaps not.

In these long centuries, she had communed with the sea. She had felt the tides within her. Understood the migration of shoals. Looked eye to liquid eye with seals. She had forgotten her name. Forgotten what it was to be human.

Almost.

Sometimes she remembered a cluster of dwellings around a well, ringed by thickets and spears. The smell of cooking. The sound of laughter. Faces that shared a look of kinship.

But that had been long ago, in another Ireland. She was a thing apart now. A mermaid. A Liban. A freak.

The monk would not come.

A year later at Larne, many gathered with Beoan on the shore. All his monks had come up from Loughbrickland. Abbot Comgall was there, too, with *his* monks. The region's king, Conaing mac Congaile, stood resplendent in a crimson cloak, surrounded by men-at-arms. The local fisherfolk chattered and pointed excitedly at the boat bobbing in the harbour. Fergus the fisherman let down his net. They all cheered.

In the months since his return from Rome, Beoan had told them all about his meeting with the mermaid.

"An angel on earth!" Abbot Comgall said. "Not because of her beauty or her song, but because she exists between worlds. Land and sea. Human and animal. The past and the present. We must listen carefully to what she has to say. It could be a message from God."

"The tail of a salmon, you say?" King Conaing wanted to know. He remembered stories he had heard around the fire on winter nights, about the Salmon of Knowledge that had made Finn wise. "Your king must hear the words of this Liban."

"But let's not forget," said a quiet monk whose name people always forgot, "that she's a person with feelings like us. We must treat her as we ourselves would like to be treated."

But everyone was too excited to listen.

Liban gasped. The shock of being hauled from the water took her breath. The fishermen were straining at the ropes. They lowered her on deck and placed her in a large tub of water. Their eyes stared back at her, like fish eyes.

"Where's the monk?" Liban looked from one man to the next.

Fergus pointed. "Monks are all ashore." He said nothing more. He and his men rowed in awed silence.

So many folk! Their faces came into focus as the boat neared land. Were they all here for her? Liban clasped her pet otter to her chest for comfort. It wriggled, especially when the tub was heaved ashore by the men. But then it stilled, a comforting warmth over her heart.

Beoan came running to meet her.

"Welcome, welcome!" He beamed all over his shaven face. "Such an honour to have you among us. This is Abbot Comgall of Bangor. And this nobleman is Conaing mac Congaile, chief of the Úi Chonaing."

Liban sat up straighter.

"He wears a red cloak!"

Conaing chuckled and stroked his beard.

"Do you want it, little maid? You shall have it."

"No." Liban's eyes seemed to look through him. "But Eochaid wore a red cloak like that."

A murmur ran through the waiting crowd.

"Tell us about Eochaid, we beg you," said Beoan.

Liban swallowed. It had been so long since she had spoken with human folk. She closed her eyes, the better to see the past, and not the rows of staring eyes.

"I was the daughter of Eochaid," she said. "There were many of us: my sister Airiu, my brothers Conaing and Curnan, and more beside. Our mother had been Eochaid's stepmother, and they had eloped together. The god Aengus himself gave them a giant horse with which to carry their goods. But Aengus said they must not let him stop on the way, lest the place of his stopping should prove fatal.

"But he did stop, at a place ringed by bramble bushes. And where he stopped, a spring of fresh water came up. Eochaid made that place his dwelling, and built a well over the spring, with a stone on top and a woman to guard it.

"One night, the woman failed to replace the stone properly. The floodwaters came up and drowned the whole place, expanding and expanding until Lough Neagh was formed. Most of my family drowned too, but I lived on beneath the waters of the lough, for a year and a day, with my little dog beside me.

"I prayed for freedom, and freedom came, but in a strange form. I became a mermaid, able to escape the loch and swim the seas. My dog became an otter and swam beside me. And so it has been from that time until this. There is no place for me among humankind. I cannot become what I once was."

"But..." King Conaing twisted hanks of beard in his fingers. "Your brother Conaing...he must have survived. Conaing, son of Eochaid, was my ancestor. We are kin. Family."

Liban swallowed hard. "Kin..." Could it be true? She had living relatives after all these years? "In that case, I bless you for it, my lord. May you and yours always be victorious."

The otter had had enough of being held. It wriggled from Liban's grasp and ran between Conaing's feet. Without thinking, one of his men-at-arms stepped forward and thrust his spear into it.

Liban gave a shriek that went like needles through the ears of everyone present.

"I curse you!" she screamed at the warrior. "You have slain the only friend I had for three hundred years. May you only ever triumph over ignoble foes. May you have no valour for the rest of your life."

The horrified man fell to his knees and crossed himself. "Forgive me," he muttered. "Forgive me."

Beoan shuffled closer and took her hand. His skin was strangely dry and warm.

"I'm sorry. I never meant for that to happen. Come with us to the monastery. You'll have new siblings. Spiritual siblings. New friends."

"That's right," said Comgall. "If you'll come to Bangor..."

"Excuse me, but I saw her first," said Beoan. "She'll be baptised at Loughbrickland, if anywhere."

Comgall gave him a chastening look. "She was found within my field-of-care. Surely that makes me her spiritual father."

"Well, it was my boat she was caught in," said Fergus the fisherman.

"What has that to do with it?" said Beoan.

Fergus crossed his muscular arms. "Did not Our Lord say, I will make you fishers of men? I think you'll agree I carried that out quite literally today. I deserve to be godfather, at least."

"So you shall be," said Comgall. "In Bangor."

They were about to break out arguing again when the quiet monk whose name no one remembered tugged on Comgall's sleeve.

"Pardon me for interrupting, but Liban belongs to no one. We can't argue over her like she's a piece of property. She's a person with feelings, just like us. And she's just been *bereaved*."

The two abbots looked shamefaced.

"You're right. It's not very saintly behaviour."

"She hasn't even said yes to baptism yet."

Abbot Comgall cleared his throat. "It should be your decision. You can come with us to...well, to wherever God decides, and be baptised into a new family. Or you can return to the freedom of the sea. We won't force you either way." He looked sidelong at Beoan. "Will we?"

Liban hesitated. "Will baptism make me human again?"

Comgall and Beoan exchanged glances.

"It will guarantee your eternal soul..." Comgall's voice wavered.

"But not the eternal body I have now." Liban thought she understood. "I will become mortal and die."

"It's a possibility," Beoan admitted.

Liban closed her eyes again and thought for a long time. The sea had been full of wonders. She would miss the dark of the ocean depths as sorely as she missed her otter companion. But if she could feel she belonged again, even for one moment...

She took a deep breath. "I'll go with you," she said.

She rode to her baptism in a chariot pulled by stags. Beasts of ancient wisdom, they came from the forest as if summoned by angels. And they pulled Liban, not to Bangor nor to Loughbrickland, but to Lough Derg, to a place that would later be called Saint Patrick's Purgatory. There, they all gathered round the holy waters. Conaing and Fergus stood as godparents. Comgall performed the baptism. Beoan assisted.

The water of the baptistery was sweet, not salt. It felt strange on Liban's flesh. She was becoming a new creation.

"What name will you take?" Comgall asked gently. He couldn't christen her 'mermaid'.

Liban gazed about her, helpless. She didn't know any Christian names.

A whisper of inspiration came to Comgall's ear.

"Muirgen, I baptise you. Born of the sea. Traverser and wonder of the ocean."

The water covered her.

People later spoke of miracles at Lough Derg. They talked about Saint Muirgen, the mermaid saint, who had come from the water with wisdom and words of prophecy. Far from being an outcast, she was a beloved Irish saint, of whom it was sung,

> My God loved Muirgen,
> A miraculous triumphant being.

Robert Hawker:

The Eccentric

Robert Hawker:

The Eccentric

In the early nineteenth century, a mermaid was seen off the coast of Bude in Cornwall. For several nights in a row, local fisherfolk heard an eerie wailing coming from the far end of the breakwater. They strained their eyes to see what was making the sound. There sat a strange creature covered in seaweed. With one hand it combed its long, green hair; with the other it held a mirror to the moon. When they tried to get near, it plunged into the waves and vanished.

Except it wasn't a mermaid. It was a young man named Robert Stephen Hawker.

He was playing a student prank. Yet, like Muirgen, Robert was a misfit. Too earthy and unconventional for Oxford academics; too cultured and artistic for the Cornish fisherfolk he served as a parish priest. He found kindred with his Celtic forerunner, Morwenna of Morwenstow. With her brother Nectan, she had come from Wales and built a prayer cell on the cliff. Following her example, Robert built a hut from driftwood. There he would sit with his opium pipe, musing over poetry and watching the sea for ships.

The Cornish coast at Morwenstow was as forbidding in Robert's day as it had been in Morwenna's. On stormy days, you could only reach the church door by clambering up the churchyard, clinging to the tombstones. A wild stretch of rocky moorland fell sharply towards the sea-battered cliffs. Many and many a ship was wrecked on that coast. Well might the locals fear the siren song of the mermaid!

Hard as rocks were those Morwenstow folk when Parson Hawker first came to them in 1835. And hard they must be, with cruel landlords and starvation wages as their lot. Those were the days when a man sold his wife for a shilling at Bideford market. Food was in short supply. Wrecking and smuggling was a way of life.

There hadn't been a vicar in Morwenstow for over a hundred years. And who would want one? Poor women must curtsy to the parson's wife on a Sunday. Labouring folk must let the squire, farmers, tradesmen and shopkeepers all go ahead of them to the communion rail, while they traipsed behind in ragged clothes. Far better to be a Dissenter!

Into this community came Robert Hawker.

Robert Hawker, who refused to wear a clergyman's sombre black. Instead, he wore the fisherman's jersey and sea boots of his parishioners; with a brown cassock he said was the colour of the Saviour's hair; and sometimes a purple cloak or a yellow horsehair poncho he called the Habit of Saint Morwenna.

Robert Hawker, who spoke out against the Poor Law that would send folk to the workhouse. Who went out in lean times with meat pies, wine, pudding and mutton for the cottagers. Who would give the blanket off his own bed, if need be.

Robert Hawker, whose first act was to fund the building of a badly needed bridge, mainly from the purse of his wealthy wife.

Folk found him unusual, that is true, but Morwenna would not have found him so. Like the Celtic saints, he was close to animals. His dog and nine cats would follow him to church, and often form his congregation. His pet black pig, Gyp, went with him on house visits, and was better behaved than many humans. His pet stag, Robin, was said to have pinned an unwanted visitor to the ground, despite being otherwise tame. And he taught that birds are the thoughts of God.

Like the Celtic saints, too, he grew his own wheat, barley and clover. No mean feat on that windswept coast! He raised pigs, poultry, chickens and ducks.

He had seen Morwenna, he said, in visions. "She loved the things of God more than the things of Men. And then the wild Atlantic rolled against the cliffs as now, and the gorse flamed over them as now... And there were men and women where you dwell as now, and there were little children on their knees as now."

The villagers could only nod.

*

32

The wild Atlantic beat against the cliffs with a fury, the night Parson Hawker was roused from his sleep.

"There's dead men on vicarage rocks," the messenger said. "A wreck. A bad one."

Robert wrapped his dressing gown tightly around himself.

"I'm coming," he said. "Remember what I've told you. No one is to profit from a wreck unless we help the survivors and give the dead a Christian burial."

The messenger nodded, grimly. It wasn't unknown for the drowning to be helped on their way to the next world, so that those on shore could benefit from the cargo.

When Robert reached the shore, the waves were tossing with broken fragments of rigging and sail. Two dead lay on the beach, stiff as the wooden figurehead that had washed ashore. As another wave lifted, a human hand reached upwards. Lifeless.

There was one survivor. The rest were carried to church, where a motherly woman laid them out for burial. When the storm abated, they were laid to rest, and their graves dressed with flowers. The figurehead of their ship – the *Caledonia* – was set up as a tombstone. It would mark the resting place of many a poor sailor pulled from the sea in Parson Hawker's time.

The Hungry Forties caused misery across Europe. Poor harvests. Potato blight. High prices. Low wages. Morwenstow's good harvest of 1843 felt like a miracle.

"We must celebrate," Robert told the people. "Cry the neck. Sing and dance. And bring your produce to church. We'll make the communion bread with the first cut of the corn. A thank-offering, just like they did in the Bible."

Was it strange for folk to bring vegetables to a church that already had a congregation of cats? If those in other places thought it strange, they soon changed their minds. It wasn't long before every parish church in the land had an annual harvest festival, like that of Robert Hawker.

It wasn't easy for Robert, though. Flamboyant on the outside, with his red trousers and pink hat, on the inside he was often lonely and depressed. As he grew older, he became increasingly addicted to opium.

Nowadays, he would probably be diagnosed as bipolar.

This was the man who had won the poetry prize at Oxford. Whose writing was admired by Charles Dickens and Sir Walter Scott. Whom Tennyson said had beaten him at his own game. For Robert Hawker published *The Quest of the Sangraal* long before the poet laureate completed *Idylls of the King*.

But who was there to appreciate his work in a Cornish fishing village? Who would understand his poet's heart; his love for legends and the old ways; his belief that the Church of Christ surpassed the rival dogmas of Anglican, Catholic and Dissenter?

Perhaps only his guardian angel. And Saint Morwenna, to whom he never ceased to speak, and for whom he named his first daughter.

Yet he was wrong to think the Cornish folk had no appreciation for his poetry. 'Trelawny' or 'The Song of the Western Men', written when he was still a student capable of dressing as a mermaid, is now the national anthem of Cornwall. And when many a conventional priest is forgotten, Robert Hawker is remembered and loved. Nowhere more so than at his driftwood hut, like the cell of Saint Morwenna, that still looks out over the wild Atlantic.

Marinos:

The Trans Monk

Marinos:

The Trans Monk

In a rock-hewn monastery in Lebanon's Qadisha Valley, a monk lay dying.

His name was Marinos. He was one of those who would later be revered as the Desert Elders: pioneers of monasticism who took to the lonely places of the Middle East after Christianity became a state religion in the reign of Emperor Constantine. Their influence was at this very time spreading west, through men like Ninian and Patrick, to the diverse peoples of the British Isles.

But Marinos' fellow monks were about to discover something different about him. Different, but by no means unique among the annals of those desert communities. Many other names have come down the centuries with similar stories. Yet that didn't lessen the shock for the brothers who found Marinos lying cold in his cell, and began the heavy task of preparing his body for burial. As they stripped away the clothes, a cry went up.

"Lord have mercy! Brother Marinos was a woman!"

Let us begin at the beginning.

A couple named Baddoura and Eugenius gave birth to a daughter, who they named Marina. Sadly, Baddoura died young, so Eugenius brought up his daughter alone.

When she reached the age of maturity, Eugenius announced his intention to give up his worldly life and enter the monastery of Qannubin.

"It's for the sake of my soul," he said heavily. "I hate to leave you, but I need to do this. Naturally, all my inheritance goes to you."

Marina looked aghast.

"What about *my* soul? What if I need you here?"

Eugenius put a hand on Marina's shoulder.

"You have your whole life ahead of you. Marriage. Children. My time has passed. I've tried to go on without your mother, but there's nothing left for me here. You're old enough to take care of yourself now."

Marina's face hardened.

"And what if that's not the right life for me either? Father, don't go alone. I'm coming with you."

Eugenius sighed.

"Do you not hear me, Marina? I'm becoming a monk. A girl can't come with me. Maybe you're too young to understand. The temptations..."

"No, Father, you don't understand. Listen to me. The one who saves a soul is like the one who created it. From now on, I am a new creation. Not Marina, but Marinos. Give my women's clothes to the poor and cut my hair. From today, I am your son."

Did Eugenius suspect that Marinos had been hiding within his daughter all this while? For he did not object to the plan. All he said was, "Take care, my child. You will be walking through fire."

And with that, the two set out for the forbidding yet holy valley near the Forest of the Cedars of God. Here are dizzying cliffs sculpted by time, where only the most tenacious of trees may grow. Here are caves where the ancients buried their dead. And here – carved from the living stone – is the monastery of Qannubin, where the Abba welcomed Eugenius and Marinos into the religious life.

Marinos soon took to a life of prayer and fasting. In this lonely place, no one knew he had once been known as Marina. He could be himself. From time to time, a brother monk would remark upon his high-pitched voice and beardless face. But someone else would say, "He's a eunuch, obviously," or, "I've heard excessive fasting stunts development."

Sadly, Eugenius did not live long at the monastery. He had come there to bury his grief, and soon he was buried too. But Marinos stayed on, taking lifelong vows to serve God and his new brothers.

About forty brothers lived communally at Qannubin. But the monastery also supported a number of hermits living in scattered caves. It was the duty of the Abba to select four brothers each month to make the round trip to visit these hermits with food. As it was a long journey, they always stayed at an inn overnight, where the innkeeper was happy to offer them refreshment.

One month, Brother Marinos was selected for the party. They visited their hermit brethren as usual, and stayed the night at the inn.

They were not the only guests. Among those drinking the innkeeper's wine was a soldier. His eye had fallen on the innkeeper's daughter, and not with gentleness. Before the girl could prevent it, he had her up against the wall by the latrine. When she tried to cry out, he clapped a dirty hand over her mouth.

"Don't you dare speak of this," he growled in her ear. "And if by some ill chance you get with child, you don't mention my name. You say it was that pretty-boy monk, that Marinos. You understand?"

The girl nodded, dumb.

In the morning, the soldier had gone, and so had the monks. But a part of the soldier remained behind. And when it grew in the girl's belly, so large she could not hide it, she was forced to confess to her father.

"It was the monk, Marinos," she stammered. Even now, she feared the soldier's sour breath and squeezing hand.

"Was it now?" Her father's voice was dangerously low. "We'll see about that."

He marched the steep path to the monastery, dragging his daughter behind him. And she burning with shame all the while.

He beat on the wooden doors.

"Where's that two-faced liar? That so-called Christian?"

People who had come to the monastery for alms and healing turned around and stared.

The innkeeper carried on shouting.

"Where is he? Bring him out?"

A face appeared at the door.

"What's all this noise? This is a place of prayer."

The innkeeper spat on the ground. "So much for your God and your prayers! I curse the hour I ever allowed a monk into my inn."

The Abba was quickly sent for.

"What is this commotion, my friend? What's wrong?"

The innkeeper thrust his pregnant daughter forward.

"See what your monk Marinos has done to my daughter! Is this what you call Christian charity? My only daughter and the prop of my old age!" He began to weep tears of rage.

The Abba blanched.

"He's not here at the moment, but when he returns, I will deal with him most severely. Believe me."

So it was that Marinos returned to Qannubin, not to a welcome but to the Abba hauling him furiously aside.

"Is this how you behave yourself the first time I let you out? Seducing the innkeeper's daughter so he comes here and makes a scene before all the lay people! It could be years before people around here trust us again."

Marinos' mind raced. How could he prove his innocence? Lift his habit and show the Abba that he lacked the necessary equipment? He would rather die! His life as a monk, his very identity would be in tatters. No. Someone had committed this crime. And the girl was too scared to say who it was. If Marinos was a true monk, his concern must be for the girl's safety and the mission of the monastery.

He knelt in the dust.

"Forgive me, Father. Like all humans, I have gone astray."

The Abba threw him out of the monastery.

Yet Marinos did not leave. God had called him to be a monk; he believed that in his heart. He stayed in the inhospitable yet holy valley near the Forest of the Cedars of God. He found a natural cave near the gates of the monastery and continued the daily pattern of prayer, despite the heat and the cold. And when folk asked what he did there, he replied, "I was expelled from the monastery for committing fornication. This is my penance."

He did not live alone for long. Less than a year had passed before the innkeeper arrived at the entrance to Marinos' cave, a swaddled bundle in his arms.

"This is your child, monk. The product of your sins. Take it."

He thrust the baby at Marinos and departed.

What could Marinos do? He couldn't abandon the innocent child to starve. He asked the local shepherds for some milk, and fed the baby, as tenderly as a mother. He changed the child's dirty cloths, and sang him to sleep with night-time psalms. All while continuing to perform the daily office.

Three years passed in this way. The child became sturdy and ran around on his little legs. Marinos had to fashion a harness to stop him tumbling off the cliff.

Inside the monastery, a group of brothers went to the Abba.

"Surely Marinos has been punished enough. He confessed his error and has done penance before the whole community. How can we ask forgiveness for our daily sins and expect pardon when he is out there, suffering? Conscience demands that we should leave too, if he is not restored."

It was not what the Abba wanted to do. But he went to the monastery gate and spoke to Marinos.

"Because of your brothers' love for you, I invite you back into the monastery. But know that you will be expected to perform the meanest chores."

"It is enough for me to live under your roof," Marinos replied.

So Marinos worked in the monastery, clearing out the night soil, scrubbing the floors, swabbing festering wounds in the infirmary. And all this while his adopted son followed at his heels, wailing for food and attention.

To the amazement of all, Marinos fulfilled his roles as both a monk and a parent. His son grew up to take vows of his own. Marinos grew older, a beloved member of the community. He was the first person to whom people turned in times of illness or distress; his prayers always seemed to exude healing and tranquillity.

And then he died.

"Lord have mercy on us, Abba. Brother Marinos was a woman!"

"What?"

The Abba rushed to the cell where the body of Marinos was laid out for burial. Sure enough, the body had the intimate parts, not of a man, but a woman.

A terrible realisation came over the Abba.

"God forgive me, I have sinned! I have wronged an innocent person."

He fell to his knees, his head drooping over the bed, and wept hot tears. For many hours, he could not be moved.

Eventually, the brothers gently asked if they could take the body. The Abba looked up from his vigil of shame. His eyes were red, and his voice was hoarse with praying.

"How can I be forgiven, when I would not forgive? I will stay here at his holy feet until I die."

"You acted in ignorance," one of the brothers said. "And you could still make restitution."

The Abba saw the wisdom of this. He sent for the innkeeper and his daughter. Years of silent shame had changed the once beautiful girl. Her shoulders were hunched, and deep lines marked her face.

"Brother Marinos is dead," the Abba told them.

The innkeeper nodded, grimly. "May God forgive him, for I cannot. He did my family a great wrong."

"It is we who have done him a great wrong," the Abba said.

He explained to the innkeeper and his daughter about Marinos' body. "So there is no way he could have committed the assault."

The innkeeper's daughter fell to her knees. Years of sobbing burst from her.

"It was a soldier," she wept. "He threatened me. He said he would hurt me unless I said it was Marinos."

The Abba laid a hand on her head.

"Much hurt has been done here. Let us pray for forgiveness together."

As they prayed, it was as if the gentle presence of Brother Marinos stood among them once more. A healing aura flooded the room. When the innkeeper's daughter stood up again, her shoulders were straighter, her face more relaxed.

"Will you tell the boy?" the innkeeper asked.

"Your grandson is now a full member of Qannubin monastery. The monks are his brothers. And Marinos was both father and mother to him. Let it remain so."

History never tells how Marinos' son reacted to the news of the unexpected body revealed in death. Perhaps he already knew. After all, he and Marinos had spent nearly three years together in the cave. To him, Marinos was simply a parent. The person who raised him and loved him, and was loved in return.

Marinos was buried with due ceremony, embalmed in myrrh. All secrecy was over. The people knew of Marinos' feminine body and masculine soul. An old saying went:

> The apparel of Marinos testifies to Marina;
> The burial of Marina shows Marinos.

The relics of his sacred body lay for years in a glass coffin, beneath a picture of him teaching his infant son.

Let all who find themselves unfairly outside the gates of fellowship draw healing from the tale of Brother Marinos and the Abba of Qannubin. Let us see him sitting calmly among us with his son in his arms, saying, "The one who saves a soul is like the one who created it."

Neot:

The Short Statured Saint

Neot:

The Short Statured Saint

It was a rainy night in Glastonbury, and the wind was blowing under the door. Brother Neot felt it more than most. Not only because he was twice as short as the other monks in the abbey. But because it was his job to guard the door at night.

Glastonbury Tor was virtually an island; only a narrow causeway connected it to the surrounding land. It was a thin place, a sacred place. But that would not keep out raiders: Danes, disaffected thegns, the desperate and the determined. The abbey's jewelled crosses and sacred vessels would draw them like a siren's song across the water. After all, Glastonbury had the most famous chalice in history. The Holy Grail. Or so it was said. Neot had never seen it, but the rumour drew people nonetheless. Hence the locked door. Hence Brother Neot's vigil.

He was no mean man, Brother Neot. He came from lordly stock. The ring-givers; the renown-winners. People even whispered that he was brother to King Alfred the Great. But because of his small stature, the only job the abbey could find him was as doorkeeper to the sanctuary. So there he waited, this wet and windy night, muttering Psalm Eighty-four to himself and trying to stay awake.

I would rather be a doorkeeper in the house of my God than dwell in the tents of wickedness. For the Lord God is a sun and shield...

A sudden hammering upon the great oak door.
"Sanctuary! For the love of God, sanctuary!"
Neot fumbled for the iron keyring that hung from his belt of rope.
"I'm coming! I'm coming!"
The hammering grew frantic.

"Hurry up! They're following!"

Neot hurried to the door. His heart was hammering in time to the strangers' knock.

"Peace be with you," he managed to say. "I am Brother Neot. Who is it that seeks sanctuary this night?"

Let it not be a murderer, he thought. Not while everyone is sleeping.

"Please, for the love of God," came the first voice. "There are robbers behind us. They've got knives."

"We're merchants," said the second. "They tried to rob us of our goods, but we resisted. They're coming! They're coming!" His voice rose to a shriek.

"Fear not," said Neot. "I have the key right here."

He lifted it towards the door. Then he froze.

His stool.

Being of short stature, he couldn't reach the keyhole unaided. One of the lay sisters, who worked in the forge, had made him an iron stool, good and sturdy. Standing on that, he could reach the keyhole without fear of falling.

But it wasn't there.

"They're coming up the hill!" the merchants yelled. They began hammering again, as if they could knock through.

Neot stood frozen. Where was his stool?

Oh, God, come to my aid. Oh, Lord, make haste to help me.

That was it! It had been his turn to officiate at Mass. He needed the stool in order to reach the altar. He must have left it there.

"Hold on. I'll be back in a minute," he said.

"What? We don't have a minute!" the second merchant shrieked. "They're in the compound. I can see their torches."

"Open the door, man!"

What could Brother Neot do? It was all in the hands of God now. He closed his eyes and slowed his breathing, as he had been taught to do in contemplation.

You did command peace; you did give peace; you did bestow peace.

He took another deep breath, ignoring the merchants' frantic cries.

An image came to Neot's mind. A well of clear, blue water. And swimming in the well, three fish with silver scales. They circled and looped around one another as they swam. An endless dance of grace and beauty.

Neot heard the voice of an angel whisper in his ear.

"These fish shall be your food all the days of your life. Take one each day, and their number shall never grow less. Three they shall be, and three remain."

Three in one and one in three.
The mighty power of the Holy Trinity.

Neot stretched out his hand and put the key in the lock.

He put the key in the lock.

Did he find the strength to stretch just a little higher? Was he able to jump? Years later, folk would claim that the lock had moved down to meet Brother Neot's hand. Perhaps it did. Who can say?

All the terrified merchants knew was that the key turned in the lock and the church door swung open. They rushed inside, not a moment too late. And maybe it was they who helped Brother Neot lock the door behind them, so that when the robbers arrived, they were safe inside. Safe from harm and persecution, in that place where even the swallow could find a home for her nest.

After that, Brother Neot was a hero. A saint. He went eventually to live as a hermit, ten miles from Bodmin. Many tales were told about him: how he ploughed his field with stags; how a huntsman on meeting Neot hung up his quiver forever; how he retrieved his shoe from a fox's mouth. It seems he was always on the side of the hunted and persecuted, as he had been that night in Glastonbury. Doubtless, he had experienced his own share of persecution, as a person of small stature.

But he was never powerless, for he drew inwardly on that deep well, and fed daily on that food that could never diminish. Solid as an iron stool, trusty as a key.

Three in one and one in three.
The mighty power of the Holy Trinity.

Brigid:

The Time Traveller

Brigid:

The Time Traveller

The midwinter solstice is a liminal time. A threshold time. A time at the crossroads between dark and light, life and death. A time when the old dies that the new may be reborn.

Brigid knew all about thresholds. She had been born out of wedlock – the child of a bondswoman and a chieftain – on the threshold of the house, just as the sun was rising. A time and a place and a person at the crossroads. So she was named Brigid, after the triple-aspected goddess of the crossroads worshipped by her people.

Now she was at another crossroads, sitting at another threshold. The sacred grove of Kildare. The church of the oaks. Here she had been trained in the lore and practice of the druids. As a druid, Brigid knew the power of the oak. It is a door to the spiritual realm, allowing one to see things that are presently hidden from view. And the solstice is the door of the year, when the Holly King concedes power to the Oak King once more, and the light begins to return.

But Brigid and her druid people had embraced the Way of Christ. The woman named for the triple goddess now worshipped the all-encompassing Trinity. The nemeton had become a monastery. And the arch-druid was now an abbess: some said a bishop, or even an apostle.

Yet much remained the same. Brigid still knew how to make a shamanic journey. She could meditate her way into a deep trance that took her into altered states of reality. It was a source of healing and transformation, both for herself and her community.

So here Brigid sat beneath the sacred oaks, her legs crossed, her palms open. She let herself forget the chill wind's bite and the aching cold of the frozen ground. She closed her eyes and asked herself: What do I seek?

She thought about the winter solstice. Not only did the light of the sun begin to wax once more, and life flow back into the oaks as the earth breathed out. Christ – the Sun of Suns and King of Kings – entered the world's darkness and breathed out the eternal Word of God.

She thought about herself: Brigid. Named for one who – in her aspect as goddess of hearth and home – played a role in healing, midwifery and the care of flock and herd. Whose own feast of Imbolc – the early spring season following midwinter – meant 'ewe's milk'. What role was there for Brigid at this threshold season? What could she do to bring life and nourishment to the people of Kildare?

She sunk deeper into a trance. The Third Eye opened behind her closed lids. It looked to Brigid like a portal opening in the trunk of the oak tree. A pulsating circle of orange and violet light stretched to become a tunnel. Brigid stood. She took three steps forward until she stood at the threshold to the portal.

She stepped through.

For some minutes, she walked an invisible path, with nothing but orange and violet light arching above her head, curving beneath her feet. The tunnel's exit grew larger and clearer. A sky full of stars. The flicker of solitary oil lamps. Square, flat-roofed houses. The bleat of sheep, a clamour of human voices, the smell of cooking fires, human and animal bodies... And the unmistakable, iron tang that flows from a woman's womb.

The next moment, she was within the crowded little room. The labouring mother grasped the horns of a ewe as she strained through a contraction. She was young, Brigid noted. This was probably her first birth. Sweat beaded the girl's forehead and stained her tunic. Two other women squeezed through the open doorway, scolding sheep out of the way. They were speaking a tongue Brigid didn't know, yet she found she could understand it. The older of the two women was carrying a bowl of water, the other clean linen. The younger one knelt at the feet of the labouring woman.

"We've brought you some..."

To Brigid's shock, the older woman snatched at her companion's arm and yanked her away.

"Don't touch! She's unclean."

"But she needs help." The younger woman looked confused. "We're all unclean once a month and during childbirth."

"I don't mean that. I mean…" The older woman lowered her voice. "Morally unclean." Brigid saw her mouth the word. "Illegitimate."

A flush came to Brigid's face. She deliberately kept her breathing slow so the vision would not fade. That could be my mother, she thought. That child could be me.

The two women left; their quarrelling faded into the night. Brigid crept closer. She now understood her part in this journey.

"Don't fear. I'm a midwife," she said to the struggling girl. "May I look and see how far along you are? I'll be gentle."

"Thank you," the girl gasped. Her eyes were bright and unfocused. Those two heartless women had given her nothing for the pain.

Brigid spread one of the linen cloths over the dirt and straw of the floor, and eased the girl onto it, then carefully raised her skirt. No wonder the poor girl was in pain! She was scarcely open.

"Is this your first?" Brigid asked.

The girl nodded.

Brigid sucked her lips. "We have some hard work ahead of us. I cannot lie. What I see here, I have usually only seen in a virgin."

"I am a virgin," the girl murmured.

Brigid's heart stopped. The winter solstice. A birth surrounded by livestock. A virgin mother.

"What's your name, my dear?" Brigid strove to keep her voice level.

"Mara."

Brigid crossed herself. Our Lady Saint Mary! Now the full meaning of the vision was apparent. Brigid was to assist in birthing the Christ of Exceeding Brightness! She pushed up her sleeves and shoved a sheep away from the water bowl.

"Mara, I need you to take a deep breath."

It was as hard a birth as any Brigid had dealt with, but at last it was over. Brigid cleared the baby's mouth and rubbed him with a towel. It was incredible to think this was the saviour of the whole creation! He was so small and helpless.

At the first cries from tiny lungs, a man pushed his way through the bleating crowd. His tired eyes and anxious features made Brigid feel sure he was the baby's father. Saint Joseph.

"Is he delivered?" Joseph asked.

"He is. Safe and healthy."

Joseph took the newborn in his arms and sung a prayer.

"His name is Yeshua," Joseph said. "The Deliverer."

I have delivered the Deliverer, Brigid thought. I have brought light into the world on this, the darkest night.

"Hold him until the afterbirth comes. Then give him to his mother. He needs milk," Brigid said.

But the young mother was too exhausted by her labours. The baby would not latch.

What can I do? Brigid thought.

She remembered her original question. What could she do to bring life and nourishment to the people? A swell in her bosom answered her. Ewe's milk. Brigid of the flocks. She herself would nurse the child, as she nourished the people of Kildare, feeding them with the pure, spiritual milk of her teaching and example. Brigid unlaced her tunic, baring her breast to the infant saviour. She felt his hot, little breath and hard, little gums. Desperate searching gave way to the rhythm of deep satisfaction. Brigid and the saviour were one.

She came back into herself, seated in the church of the oaks. There was frost on the roots. Her legs were numb. But beyond the bare branches, the sky was a cascade of silver dust. The Christ of Exceeding Brightness was born anew at the crossroads this solstice night.

Quiteria:

The Nonuplet Warrior

Quiteria:

The Nonuplet Warrior

I n the state of Tamil Nadu in southern India, a shrine to Saint Quiteria stands in the church at Kuthenkuly. It is a place of devotion, and of miracles.

On the other side of the world, in the state of Bahia in Brazil, a statue stands of a young woman who fought for her people's freedom: Maria Quiteria, named for the saint.

Meanwhile, the church of Sainte-Quitterie in Aire-sur-l'Adour is a stopping place for pilgrims on the Camino Santiago.

What can such far-flung places have to do with a Celtic saint? And what is her story?

In Galicia – so the story goes – in the latter days of the Roman Empire, a woman gave birth to nine daughters.

In many cultures around the world, a multiple birth has been seen as uncanny. So it was in this woman's culture. She feared what people would say. Was she a beast, to give birth to a litter? Had she slept with multiple men?

In the north-west corner of the Iberian peninsula, the ancient Celtic culture of the Gallaeci met with the Latin culture of the Romans. A green and rugged landscape of dolmens and healing stones, it was also a place of defensive walls, bridges and bathhouses, temples and towers. The woman's husband was a Roman military official. She had to maintain a good face before her neighbours. Nothing was more important, to Celt or Roman.

"Get rid of them," she said to her maid. "I don't care how. Drown them, like kittens. Nobody must know of this. I must have been cursed."

Such a terrible thing to say! Yet such is the power of a curse in the human mind.

The maid took the babes away. But she could not bear to drown them. Instead she gave them to a local woman, to raise as her own. The woman was glad to do so. She was a Christian, you see, and understood that by taking in strangers, you may entertain angels unaware.

In this belief, she wasn't far from the truth.

The girls grew and became strong. Their names were Eumelia and Liberata, Gema and Genebra, Germana and Basilica, Marica and Vitoria. And the eldest, who was the leader of them all: Quiteria.

They grew up with the song of justice ringing in their hearts. Liberty to captives. Freedom for the oppressed. Good news for the poor. The Roman Empire may have been all-powerful, but they had faith in a much greater kingdom.

It seems that, by some means, their father recognised them. Perhaps he saw the family resemblance. Perhaps his wife confessed the truth. Perhaps the foster family sought him out, needing his financial provision and social connections for the girls' future.

At any rate, they were restored to their true family. But it was not a happy reunion. Their father worshipped the Roman gods – including the emperor himself. Christianity was a dangerous religion, conducive to public disorder. His daughters, now he had them, would be drawn back into civilisation and wed to Roman officers.

The daughters refused.

Is it surprising they would resist the authority of a family that had rejected them for existing? Is it surprising they would cling to a church in which there was neither male nor female, slave or free?

Their father locked them in a tower.

Perhaps it was the lighthouse, or one of the many Roman fortifications that still stand in Galicia. It must have been a regular place of imprisonment, for the sisters were not the only inmates.

It was then that Quiteria hatched her plan.

"We will not allow ourselves to be kept down, sisters," she said. "We will fight to free ourselves, our fellow captives, and the Galician people. Rome does not hold sway over us. We have a greater Lord!"

And that is what they did. They broke everyone out of prison, and fought Rome as guerrillas among the hills of Galicia and Gaul, until Quiteria was beheaded as a martyr.

Some even say she walked with her own head, to choose the place of her burial.

Incredible? Ridiculous?

Or perhaps the story goes like this:

Quiteria was the leader of a women's fighting force. A sisterhood run by women, for women. Together, they raised the sword of justice, and freed the downtrodden. They gave women agency over themselves. They gave the ordinary people dignity in the face of Rome's might.

And the establishment didn't like it.

But such freedom cannot be stopped. Cut off the head – cut down the leader – and the body she empowered will keep on walking.

That is the true legacy of Quiteria.

In nineteenth-century Brazil, Maria Quiteria was inspired to take up arms and join the fight to liberate her people from imperial power. In India, Tamil Christians have worshipped and been blessed in fellowship with Quiteria for several centuries. And pilgrims on the Camino Santiago find strength to keep walking in the church that bears her name.

Keep walking; keep fighting.

Freedom will come.

Melangell:

The Protector of Hares

Melangell:

The Protector of Hares

A prince was once hunting in a green valley.
The name of the prince was Brochwel Ysithrog, Prince of Powys. A boar of a man. He was famed among the Britons as a warrior; fiercely holding out against the invading Mercians. He ruled from Shrewsbury, known in those days as Pengwern. So great was he that the immortal Taliesin was his bard for a time, singing his praise in the Land of Brochwel. Who would gainsay such a man? Surely it would take a giant from the age of Brutus! Or a hero from the pages of the *Mabinogion*!

In actual fact, it was someone much smaller.

Brochwel was coursing hares that day. His dogs led the pursuit deeper and deeper into the valley; a real-life game of hares and hounds! Following the course of the stream called the Afon Tanat; beneath the shadow of Moel Dimoel, where once dwelled the giant Berwyn. The clouds grew lower and the mist grew thicker. Brochwel and his huntsmen pressed on.

The dogs were hard on the tail of the hare now. That fleet and mystical animal was in danger of being caught. It leapt for the cover of some bramble bushes. The hounds, huntsmen, and Brochwel followed.

What they saw turned them motionless as carvings on a rood screen.

A young woman was sitting amid the brambles.

Her back was straight; her posture was calm. Her clothes, though faded, were cut of good cloth and embroidered at the hems. She wore a russet cloak, pinned with a knotwork brooch. The cloak pooled on the ground about her; Brochwel could detect the trembling form of the hare disappearing beneath it.

The dogs cowered back, whimpering. The huntsmen's horns froze to their lips. Brochwel knew they expected his command, but his mouth had gone dry. The young woman's grey eyes looked into his, with dignity and determination. Brochwel wondered if he had strayed into a tale. One about ancient goddesses of the wild hunt, to whom hares ran for protection. Goddesses who could shapeshift into hares; who forbade the eating of hares as akin to eating one's own grandmother.

Then the goddess huffed. And Brochwel knew she was an ordinary maiden, after all.

"You're disturbing my contemplation." The young woman's voice was as clear as her grey eyes. And as determined.

"Ah. Well, I'm sorry about that." Something about this woman had Brochwel quite flustered. "If you'll just shoo that hare out from under your cloak, we'll be on our way."

"Absolutely not!" The young woman drew the quivering shape closer. "I came to this valley to get away from men controlling my life. I'm not about to revert now. This hare deserves to find sanctuary just as much as I do."

Brochwel scratched his beard. "I fear, madam, that we've begun on the wrong foot. Allow me to introduce myself. I am Brochwel Ysithrog, Prince of Powys. And you are...?"

"My name is Melangell," said the young woman. "Daughter to a king in Ireland. He wished to arrange a marriage for me while I was still a child. But that was not my wish." She gave a grim smile. "I came across the sea to find sanctuary and solitude. Since I came to this valley, I've managed to avoid men for fifteen years." She rolled her eyes. "Until today."

"I see," said Brochwel. "You do understand that I am lord of these lands. I could command you to leave this valley," he said. "Or to wed me."

Melangell's grey eyes bored into him.

"But I won't. Of course I won't." It was something of a relief for Brochwel to say this. "No, I grant you this valley of Cwm Pennant as your sanctuary. No one shall disturb you again."

"No," said Melangell. "They won't."

And they didn't. Pennant Melangell is still a secluded place of pilgrimage. During the remaining years of her life, Melangell offered sanctuary – not only to hares, but to women like herself, seeking a place of refuge. A monastic community of women was founded, which in time became Saint Melangell's church. Those who wrote her story said that miracles were wrought by the intercession of Melangell's hares. Perhaps that's what her sisters in the community called themselves. Like those goddesses from myths of the past, they found safety in the wild places, protected others, and were transformed.

Olcán:

The Foundling

Olcán:

The Foundling

Dalriada was an ancient Gaelic kingdom spanning both sides of the Irish Sea, by way of the Giant's Causeway. Later famed for its wars with King Bridei of the Picts under Áedán mac Gabráin – who granted Columba the Isle of Iona – in earlier times it was visited by the equally formidable figure of Patrick.

This was the Irish part of Dalriada: a small corner of Ulster, bounded on the west by the fast-flowing River Bush. Across this river came Patrick with his travelling household. His assistant bishop and priest; his Brehon lawman; his bell-ringer, psalmist and sacristan; his strong-man, whose help they would surely need to ford the river; his charioteer and horses; his cowherd and cattle. Guest-host and cook; brewer and woodman. It was like the travelling entourage of a king. And a king came forth to meet it: Doro of Carn Setna.

And one other person. A young boy called Olcán.

Doro wished Patrick to baptise the boy and take him on as a trainee priest. There were several such boys already travelling with Patrick. They studied scripture, learned to chant plainsong, and assisted the priests in their duties. It was a sought-after education for the sons of bards and chieftains.

But Olcán was not Doro's son.

He had no idea who his father was.

What had happened was this. Some time back, a woman had taken ill with a fever. She was a foreign woman, a slave perhaps, and no one took particular care to establish whether she was dead or still alive. They were afraid to catch whatever had taken her. And if she was not exactly dead now, she would be soon.

So they built a cairn of stones over her, and considered their duty done. But there was another thing they should have considered.

The woman was pregnant.

A few days later, King Doro and his druid were walking past the cairn when they heard a thin wailing from within. The king commanded that the cairn be dismantled. Inside, they found the woman, dead as the stones around her. And a naked baby, still joined by the cord, who was very much alive.

"That is bad," said the king.

The word he used for bad was 'olc'. So the druid named the child Olcán. Not a propitious name. But King Doro and his household must have cared for the child. For here was the king now, asking Patrick to take Olcán as a pupil.

"Very well," said Patrick. "I shall."

Imagine the thrill! This foundling boy with no father and no genealogy to give him status. Taken into the household of Patrick to be educated alongside boys who could trace their bardic lineage back through generations.

He must have been talented. For in time, Patrick sent him to further his education in Gaul, where Patrick himself had studied as a younger man under Martin of Tours and Germanus of Auxerre.

Picture young Olcán, raised in a land of wattle huts and ring forts, arriving in Arles, the Rome of Gaul! There was Constantine's palace with its thermal baths. There was the theatre and a huge, circular arena. There were the great schools and the highest court in the province. The forum thronged with lawyers, learned doctors, and officials of all kinds. The marketplace enticed the senses with the tastes and colours of the world.

But this would be no pleasure trip. In the monastic schools of Martin and Germanus, self-denial was the ruling virtue. While Olcán would learn from the greatest minds of Western Europe, and enjoy access to more books than filled the whole of Ireland, he would be required to sleep on bare stone and eat only the sparest of diets. Small wonder that even Patrick himself smuggled in a pork chop during his student days!

When Olcán returned, an experienced and educated monk, Patrick made him Bishop of Armoy. And he in turn educated other boys, including Mac Nissi, the man who would one day replace and surpass him.

After Olcán, Armoy was overrun by poverty, fire and slaughter. It ceased to be a bishopric, passing into the hands of the Bishops of Connor, of whom Mac Nissi was the first. Olcán left as little trace in this world as he had brought into it.

And yet – what a life! A foundling child, plucked from the lips of death, adopted into the household of Ireland's patron saint, his talents given room to thrive. And then to pay forward the benefits he had received.

He needs no greater memorial than that.

Hubert:

Hunter of the White Stag

Hubert:

Hunter of the White Stag

Many are the tales of the white stag, that visitor from the spiritual realm. From the White Stag of Bamburgh that vanished into the sea; to the Church of the White Stag in Llangar, built using mortar mixed with the stag's blood.

Many are those who are said to have hunted it. From Pwyll, Prince of Dyfed, who followed it to the otherworldly realm of Annwn; to David, King of Scotland, whose encounter led him to found Holyrood Abbey. The white stag's appearance is said to herald a new beginning, a crossing over the threshold of adventure.

This tale concerns Hubert, a Frankish nobleman in the days of Aidan and Hilda. A courtier of the Merovingian kings, he had newly married Floribanne, daughter of the Count of Leuven, and she had borne him a son named Floribert.

His joy should have been complete. But Floribanne did not survive childbed. Distraught, Hubert withdrew from court life and threw himself into his other great passion.

Hunting.

In the vast and ancient forest of the Ardennes, Hubert could give way to his most primal urges. Gone were his rings, brooches and buckles, heavy with gold and garnets. All he needed was his bow and his quiver, his horse and his hounds. The blood hot in his veins. The quarry within his sights. Predator and prey; man and beast. The oldest enmity. Farewell to the court with its cut-throat politics. Farewell to the softness of women, invading a man's heart, making him weak. As for God – huh! If he was so almighty, why did he not prevent Floribanne from dying?

So he rode into the forest. Day after day after day. His hounds hard on the scent; his beaters thrashing through the undergrowth. On his horse; off his horse. Anything so long as it wore him bone-weary by the end of the day. So he slept so hard he couldn't dream. Anything but that.

One Good Friday, Hubert rode out as usual. No matter that his men wished to pray. Sacred or profane, feast or fast, all days were alike to Hubert. No matter that custom forbade the eating of meat on the day Christ shed his blood. What about the blood of poor Floribanne, in agony on her childbed?

No, Hubert would hunt this day, as every day. The hounds soon scented a stag. Hubert saw the white of his tail as the creature broke cover. Then again, in the clearing. It was not just the stag's tail that was white. Every part of him was milk-white, from hoof to antler.

"This is no ordinary stag, my lord," one of his men told him.

But Hubert paid no heed. "I will bag this beast before the day is out. Onwards!"

Hubert, his men and hounds ran the stag hard. At last, they held it at bay. Hubert dismounted for the kill. The stag looked at Hubert and lowered its horns.

And the strangest thing happened. Between the stag's antlers, a golden glow appeared. And within that tranquil light, the crucifix.

Hubert found himself bending the knee, right there on the forest floor.

As if one miracle wasn't enough, the stag spoke.

"Hubert, son of Bertrand, your life stands at a crossroads. Keep going the way you are, and it will end in destruction."

Hubert bowed his head. He knew this reckless behaviour was a cover for his grief, and a shallow covering at that. But he couldn't face the black hollow at the centre of his soul.

"What should I do, Lord?" He felt as if the spirit of Christ was speaking through the white stag.

"Go and see Bishop Lambert. He will tell you what to do. And Hubert. Remember that we beasts do not exist simply for you to hunt. You must honour us. Know us. Listen to us. Treat us with compassion as God's fellow creatures. For truly, all life on earth exists in God. If you must hunt us, do so with dignity and respect, giving thanks for our sacrifice on your behalf. This will be your legacy to the world."

Hubert sought out Bishop Lambert as the stag instructed. He was a kind and wise mentor; a true Soul Friend. Under his guidance, Hubert found himself again, and in so doing, found his faith. In time, Hubert followed Lambert into the priesthood, becoming Bishop of Maastricht in his stead when Lambert died. Later still, he was Bishop of Liège. He was a good priest: diligent in prayer; generous to the poor. He preached the Gospel in the forest of the Ardennes, among people to whom the white stag was probably a familiar figure. They would have understood the call of Christ coming through that traditional messenger from the Otherworld, heralding a new birth.

But his lasting legacy is as the patron of ethical hunting, deer management and animal welfare. The Saint Hubert's hound – a forebear of the basset and bloodhound – was yearly presented to the king of France by the monastery of the Ardennes. A nail called Saint Hubert's Key was used to treat rabies, well into the twentieth century. And many animal charities bear Hubert's name.

As Columbanus, Irish missionary to the Franks, said, "Understand the creation if you would wish to know the Creator." For truly, all life exists in God.

Oda:

The Pilgrim

Oda:

The Pilgrim

This story begins where that of Hubert left off: in Liège, with Bishop Lambert.

Or rather, with his bones.

Lambert had died a martyr in the clash of clans: Merovingian and Carolingian, who fought for supremacy in the Low Countries in those days. Now there were miracles at his tomb. Many who had failed to find healing in other places, came to Liège with fresh hope.

One such pilgrim was named Oda. She had come, she said, from the kingdom of Dalriada, where her father ruled. He had sent her here on pilgrimage because she was blind. Her parents had walked many fruitless miles around the isles of Britain, seeking a cure. Now, word of holy Lambert had spread across the sea. And here was Oda, seeking the saint's intercession as she prayed to God for the gift of sight.

Along with many other pilgrims, she knelt in the small chapel Hubert had caused to be built over Lambert's resting place. It had been a weary journey, but now that she was here, Oda could sense tranquillity. This was a place of love and understanding. As Lambert had been a Soul Friend to Hubert in life, and helped him heal from his wife's death, so at his tomb, Oda felt him near, waiting with encouragement and good counsel.

"Bishop Lambert, pray with me to the Lord."

The words hovered in Oda's mouth. She knew why her parents had sent her here. Blind, she could not play her part in the interweaving of clans. No chieftain would take a blind wife. Sighted, she could become a woman of influence. She could advance her family's cause.

But what about me? Oda thought. She didn't need sight to make her complete. She was a child of God; she felt that more strongly than ever. Still, it would be wonderful to see the things the other pilgrims had described on their journey. Foaming waves with dolphins leaping. Valleys and hills a thousand shades of green. (What was green?) Church walls covered in painted angels. The different clothing and features of people in new lands.

Yes, I would like that, Oda thought. I would like that very much.

That night, she fell asleep beside the holy tomb. When she woke in the morning, she knew everything had changed. Light. Colour. Shapes. Hard to process at first, but gradually becoming clearer. A stone floor. Faces. A carven cross.

She could see.

She could see, but her parents could not.

"I owe God my life," she tried to explain. "I want to be a *peregrinato*: a wanderer for the love of God."

"You owe your life to me and your mother!" her father said. "Who do you think paid for your pilgrimage? Of course, we praise God for the miracle, and we mean to give generously in thanks. But your foremost act of gratitude must be to participate in the life of your people by submitting to marriage."

"That is not my vocation." Oda folded her arms. "I am called to be a pilgrim."

But her father would have none of it. His daughter was greatly desired now, throughout Argyll, Fortriu, Gododdin and Alt Clud. She would be wed, come what may.

So one night, while everyone was sleeping, Oda and one faithful maid stole away, to begin their peregrinations.

The places they went!

Down the Via Imperii to Rome, to visit the tombs of the apostles Peter and Paul, and the basilicas that Emperor Constantine had ordered to be built over them. There, so much of the ancient glory remained. There too, in those catacombs beneath the earth, a reminder of the secret lives of Christians, in the days of persecution that had sent the apostles to their deaths.

Then down into the spur of Italy's heel. To the Sanctuary of Monte Sant'Angelo, where popes and pilgrims had gone before. There, it was said, the Archangel Michael had appeared in a cave, and thrown back a herdsman's arrow. Michael had promised the people protection from their enemies, and consecrated the place for Christian worship.

What an honour for Oda and her companion, to visit such special places! What a miracle in itself, for two women to travel so far in those days!

But when seeking a place to settle, it was to Frankish territory that Oda returned. Liège and Maastricht on the River Maas. She must have felt a special affinity with the place of her healing. She and her companion chose a quiet spot near Venray, where they could live out their lives in love and friendship, with each other and with nature.

Nature loved them back. It wasn't long before birds - abundant in that marshy land of reeds and peat bogs - gathered around the moss-covered hut, waiting for crumbs and scraps. Of course, many wings flocking to one place made the local people notice they had new neighbours. Most of them left the strangers alone, since they did no harm.

But every age has its trolls, its goblins, who prey on the outsider. A group of young men from the town began to harass Oda and her friend. What did they say about two women living alone together in the wild? What did they threaten against them?

Oda didn't want to leave her home, but she felt she had no choice. It had become unbearable. She and her maid moved further south, towards Weert.

This new hut was in the middle of a moor. To protect themselves against the battering of wind, rain and snow - and against unwanted visitors - Oda planted some bushes around the perimeter. Soon, they had a fine hedge. The two companions settled down, making friends with the birds once more.

In the meantime, Oda's father, King Eochaid, had come seeking her. He could not allow the scandal of a runaway daughter to taint his clan. And he guessed she would return to the lands of Bishop Lambert.

One night, he arrived at the inn in Weert. When his party paid for food and lodging, the innkeeper examined the coins closely.

"It's a fair way you've come, I'll guess. I don't see coins of this stamp around here often. In fact, the only people who've paid me with these are the two hermit women on the moor."

Eochaid grabbed the innkeeper by his tunic lacings.

"Hermit women, you say? With coins like these?"

"Yes, and they talk like you, too."

That was all the confirmation Eochaid needed. He got directions to the hut and set out immediately.

But, unlike his daughter, Eochaid was unfamiliar with this country. He could find no easy way to the hut. The bushes forced him onto unsafe ground. And, when at last it seemed he was getting somewhere, flocks of magpies flew screeching out of the hedge, forcing him to retreat.

The nature she loved had served Oda well.

Eochaid returned home without seeing his daughter. For a time, she lived in peace. But there came a day of sadness, when Oda's beloved companion passed away. Then the moor seemed haunted by memories that stabbed. The lonely hut no longer felt safe in the depths of night when the wind howled.

So, Oda the pilgrim made her last journey, west towards Eindhoven, away from the traffic of the river, where no one could track her down. In a clearing in the woods, she made her home. And though she was lonely, she made new friends. People sought her out, asking for advice. She was a holy woman, they decided. When at last she died, they swore they saw light from heaven, as if the whole hut was on fire.

So it came about, that the home of Oda the pilgrim became a place of pilgrimage. People came there to pray for miracles, as Oda had once prayed at the tomb of Bishop Lambert. The noblewoman who owned the land had a church built on the spot. The town that grew around it still stands. It is called Sint-Oedenrode: 'Saint Oda's clearing'.

Gobnait:

Seeker After Resurrection

Gobnait:

Seeker After Resurrection

Another saint who followed the white deer was Gobnait. But she was no hunter. She was seeking her place of resurrection. She found it among the bees.

What do you do when your home is no longer a home? When arguments and rifts in the family force you to go your separate ways? Gobnait's world was one of feuds and revenge. Brother could turn against brother. Branches of the family tree could be at war for generations. A war, not of harsh words or frosty silence; but of the sword and the battle-axe, of cattle-raiding and hostage-taking. A feud could turn a place of safety into a place of danger.

So, Gobnait left the home she had known, and set out to find a new place of safety. A place to change the evil memories to good. A place of resurrection. From her native County Clare, she sailed across the sea to Inisheer, one of the Aran Islands, where Enda kept his Places of Refuge.

These were no cosy retreats. The windswept island had been divided into eight parts, each of them housing a monastic community. Gobnait came upon villages of stone cells encircling a church and a common kitchen. Those who chose to pray and study here must sleep on the cold ground. They must grow their own oats and barley, bake their own bread, tend their own flocks, and weave their own clothes. They must eat no meat and drink no wine. It was a harsh life, but a holy one; many were the saints who visited this place and drew from it inspiration. Gobnait would be another. She would learn the monastic way from Enda, and find peace on the island.

Yet, strange to tell, Gobnait found no peace.

Oh, for a while she did. She enjoyed being part of a community, and didn't mind the hardship. In fact, she learned to love the wild wind and the barren earth. But something within her was restless. A nervous energy she could not explain.

One night – the slow-falling night of summer in the north, when the clouds streamed red and gold on a low horizon, casting their fire upon the sea – Gobnait felt a spiritual presence. There in the fiery cloud, she saw a form of a six-winged creature, and heard a voice say, "This is not your place of resurrection. Get up. Follow the white deer.

Where they graze, three times three,
There shall your resurrection be."

Like all Celtic people, Gobnait knew the meaning of the white deer. A call to quest and adventure. She knew the power of three times three: no number could be stronger. Christ himself was a guest in Mary's womb for three times three months.

So she thanked Enda and his community for all they had taught her, and set out on her travels again.

Back over the sea she went, to the Irish mainland. She travelled through the province of Munster, through Waterford, Cork and Kerry, always seeking after the white deer. Many a spring she drank from – like the deer in the Psalms, whose longing for God is as a thirst – and many a holy well she left behind. But she did not find her place of resurrection.

She came to Clondrohid, north of the River Lee between Cork and Killarney. There she caught sight of the white deer: three of them. Her heart quickened; could this be the place of resurrection? But although she watched and waited, no more than three appeared. She travelled on.

North-west, following the course of the Sullane River, she came to Ballymakeery. There she saw three more white deer: six in all.

Could this be my place of resurrection? Gobnait wondered.

But although she watched and waited, there were no more deer. She travelled on.

By now she was growing weary, wondering if she had misread the signs. Should she go back to Clondrohid or Ballymakeery, and wait for more deer to arrive?

She came to the next village, a place called Ballyvourney. On a small rise overlooking the Sullane, nine white deer were grazing. The words she had hidden in her heart sang loudly:

Where they graze, three times three,
There shall your resurrection be.

Gobnait fell to her knees in gratitude.
"Thank you, Blessed Three. This is the place."

How to establish a new home as your place of resurrection? For Gobnait, it was time to leave off following the white deer, and turn her attention to a different creature. As she sought to recreate in her own way the communities she had seen on Inisheer, Gobnait considered what was needed.

Homes. Humble homes, yes; but places where her religious siblings could retreat to pray, separate yet connected. Healing. The sick should be tended here, the broken made whole. A haven. Protection within the holy village from the feuding and raiding that blighted the rest of the land. Everyone who came here should experience the deep peace Gobnait now felt.

So it was that Gobnait's mind turned to bees. Bees, who modelled hard work and community. Who inspired the beehive cells where monastic siblings lived and prayed. Bees who made honey, a source of great healing. Bees who, in a desperate hour, might be persuaded to swarm against a raiding party and keep the village safe.

Gobnait tended her bees and grew her community. She became abbess of a new religious order, dedicated to healing the sick. It was said in later days that Gobnait's prayers turned back the plague from the borders of Ballyvourney, such was her reputation as a healer. Future generations said her bees became soldiers when raiders threatened; and that the prayer bell of Saint Gobnait could bring down a castle wall. For certain, she was a warrior of the spirit, turning evil memories to good deeds.

And one year at the first quickening of the green, the time of year when candles are blessed and bees do their spring cleaning, Gobnait left this life in the company of that fiery messenger who once told her to seek the nine white deer. Ballyvourney became her place of resurrection indeed.

For Gobnait knew one more thing about bees. They are symbols of rebirth and immortality. Old tales tell how the soul may leave the body as a bee, and see many wonders. And their re-awakening from sealed wax cells is an annual rising from the tomb, a reminder of the greater resurrection to come.

It is said that, at Saint Gobnait's well in Ballyvourney, a white deer may be seen. If you see it, may it lead you to your place of resurrection. May that place be a home, a healing and a haven, like Gobnait's home among the bees.

Ronán:

The Werewolf Refugee

Ronán:

The Werewolf Refugee

It was a time when many refugees crossed the English Channel in frail craft, fleeing from war and the loss of their homes. But they were travelling south, not north. Towards the European continent, not away. Britain - the land of the Britons - was becoming Angle-land - England. The old Roman Empire was fast breaking up, and newly empowered Germanic peoples had come west, seeking riches. Forcing indigenous folk from their homes and lands. Assimilate or flee.

From Cornwall, over the sea they came, to a place on the tip of Gaul that the Romans had called Armorica. They made it a little Britain: Brittany, or Breizh. And though their new neighbours may have been distant relations, few acknowledged the connection.

One of these new Bretons was Ronán, the son of two of Patrick's converts. He came to live as a holy hermit. Dwelling in a hidden hut in the woods. Washing in spring water. Ringing his bell. Praying and fasting. Sharing the songs of the birds and the paths of the beasts.

Surely that was harmless enough?

But Brittany was the land of the werewolf and the wolfleader. Men who lived deep in the forest, served by packs of wolves at their command. Who sat on chairs of woven grass and oak branches, while wolves attended them. Men who shed their human clothing, put on a belt of wolf skin, and went forth in the shape of the *Bleiz Garv*: the Cruel Wolf. Such creatures were evil incarnate; ravaging and devouring; as cunning as they were violent. Capable of inflicting every depraved horror upon good, honest people.

Close to Ronán's hermitage, there lived a farmer and his wife. Like most people, they depended on their little flock of sheep and their little plot of crops. They didn't share Ronán's faith, a religion many had shed with the departure of the Romans. They preferred to stick to the folk-charms they knew: dancing to prepare a threshing floor, and putting out bread for the Little People. You couldn't be too careful, when Death waited at every turn.

But when a wolf came - an ordinary wolf, mind - and made off with one of the farmer's lambs, it was Ronán who came running from his hut; Ronán who rebuked the wolf, so it left with its tail between its legs, and dropped that lamb by its mother.

"How did you do that?" The farmer was enthralled. The loss of a lamb would have hit him hard. "Such authority, and over the Night Dog, too." It was ill luck in those parts to name the wolf aloud.

Ronán gave a sideways smile.

"The authority belongs not to me, but to my Lord, Jesus Christ. He is master of man and beast alike."

"If that's so, then I must serve him too," said the man.

But the farmer's wife was not so convinced. Her name was Keben.

"Are you a fool, to be taken in by this stranger, with his cross and his bell? There's only one kind of man who can command Night Dogs." She mouthed the words. "A wolfleader."

"No!" said the farmer.

But Keben was a pot on the boil now. "Think about it. He lives out in the forest, away from decent folk. He dresses in rough clothes. He performs strange rituals in a language none of us know. He's not one of us."

"He saved the lamb."

"That was just a test of his powers. The next windy night, he could summon his pack to ravage the whole flock."

"No."

"Yes. And worse than that. He could send..." Keben hissed in her husband's ear. "The *Bleiz Garv*. I wouldn't be surprised if he's a werewolf himself. He could be out there, changing his skin right now. No one in this settlement is safe!"

However much her husband argued, Keben became more and more convinced by her own story. She took to visiting the neighbours, to gossip about Ronán.

"Don't let your sons go to him for teaching. Don't let your daughters out of your sight. Who knows when he will strike next."

Soon, there was a little, chattering group of them. But others spoke up for Ronán.

"His teachings are good and peaceful."

"He healed my sore with his prayers and his herb-lore."

"His God is the god of all. Rock, river and sun. That's true power."

Keben was not a woman to be contradicted. Her neighbours were mocking her! Ronán *was* a wolfleader and a werewolf. And she would prove her point. A small deception for a greater good.

She hid her youngest child in an oaken chest, where grain for the winter was stored. Then she ran out among the flocks, shouting.

"Help! Help! The *Bleiz Garv* is among us! He has devoured my child!"

The neighbours came running. Women soon huddled around Keben, consoling her anguish, or adding to it with wailing of their own. A girl and boy ran for the village headman. Several smallholders set off for Ronán's hut, cudgels in hand.

Soon, the village counsel was assembled, with the headman in the settlement's only chair. He questioned both Ronán and Keben closely. Then he scowled.

"Where are the child's remains?"

"There were no remains. He ate her whole," Keben replied.

"Nonsense. The Night Dog always leaves remains. Bones. Clothes, at the very least. You're not telling me he ate those?"

Keben shrugged. "He must have hidden them."

Eager helpers began searching. It wasn't long before someone lifted the lid of the chest.

"I've found her! The child is here, and whole. But…" There was a horrid pause. "I don't think she's breathing."

Keben gave a shriek like a wounded animal.

"What have you done, woman?" her husband demanded.

Keben didn't answer him. "My baby!" she screeched. "My baby!"

Above the rising babble, Ronán's voice rang out.

"Give the child to me."

The headman looked at him, questioning.

"My master is the Resurrection and the Life," Ronán said. "He can raise the dead."

"Give him the child," cried Keben's husband.

Ronán took the child in his arms. He bent over her, breathed on her, uttered prayers in the name of his Lord. The little one jerked and spluttered, and then began to cry.

"A miracle!" Keben's husband fell to his knees.

The headman rose, gravely.

"From now on, we will honour Ronán and his God. No foul accusation will be brought against him again."

And so it was. Many in that place came to believe in Jesus through the witness of Ronán. But Keben never forgave him for proving her wrong. She never believed. It is said that, when Ronán died, and an ox-cart bore his body to the hermitage for burial, Keben attacked the oxen and tore off one of their horns. In that very spot, they say, Keben fell foul of an earthquake and died. Keben's Cross, the place is called, passed by pilgrims on *La Grande Tromérie* in Locronan, the part of Brittany that bears the saint's name.

Robert of Knaresborough:

The Unsettled Hermit

Robert of Knaresborough:

The Unsettled Hermit

I t took place in the days of Richard the Lionheart and his brother King John. Days of Crusades abroad and taxation at home. Days of hideous persecution for York's Jewish community. In those days, a new monastic movement swept through France and England.

It was many years since the great Anglo-Saxon monastic houses fell to the Vikings. The Norman kings were now in power. The Church was at odds with both Crown and people, corrupt and in need of reform. People needed something new. Something real.

Some embraced an alternative lifestyle. They drew their inspiration from Desert Elders like Abba Anthony, who abandoned his worldly possessions to live in a cave, striving with the elements and his own demons. They lived in chapels, in gatehouses, beside rivers, in cells attached to churches, and in caves in the forest. In twos or threes with small networks of helpers, they grew vegetables and accepted the charity of those who came to visit, seeking spiritual guidance. It wasn't a formal network, but they often knew one another, and followed a similar pattern of prayer and abstinence.

One person who felt this call to more was Robert Flower of York. He was a wealthy young man, whose father and brother both served as mayor. When he joined the Church, they may have expected him to rise to the rank of bishop. But Robert couldn't settle into a priest's life. He was no more than a sub-deacon when he made a decision.

A position in the Church shouldn't be something you get because your father is wealthy, or to reward loyalty to the king, he thought. The greatest in God's kingdom should be a servant to all.

Robert switched to life in a monastery. But he couldn't settle into that any better. Where was the adventure? The challenge?

I want to be like Abba Anthony, thought Robert. A holy hero. Living simply. Working with my own hands. Doing good to the people, not living off their labour.

So, after only eighteen weeks in the monastery, Robert was off again. This time to Knaresborough, and a cave beside the River Nidd, where a knight named Giles was living as a hermit.

"I've come to join you!" Robert picked his way carefully down the stairs in the great limestone crag. On the other side of the river, he could see Knaresborough Castle, high upon a rock. It was there that Thomas á Becket's murderers had fled when Robert was just a child.

Giles looked up and smiled uneasily. "Oh, good."

Robert reached the cave and put down his knapsack.

"Yes, I want to become your disciple. Living the full ascetic life. Out among the elements. Real spiritual warfare!"

What Robert didn't realise was that Giles was beginning to tire of the 'full ascetic life'. The cold was getting into his bones, and his gums were bleeding. He longed to sleep in a house with walls, and to eat something that had grown in a garden. Before long, he had gone back to town, and Robert was left alone.

Being a hermit was much harder than Robert imagined. The seedlings he planted washed away. Mice ate his bread. He could hear the howling of wolves at night, or the shouts and curses of outlaw men. He tried to pray, but he couldn't concentrate. He couldn't sleep either. When the poor of Nidderdale came to him for help, he didn't know what to say.

Eventually, a wealthy widow named Juliana came to his aid.

"I have a chapel on my land dedicated to Mother Hilda of Whitby. Why don't you make that your hermitage? You'll have a bit of land to farm, and you'll be under my protection."

Robert sighed. It felt like defeat. But Juliana was insistent.

"You'll be no good to the poor, wasting away in that cave. Come where it's safe."

But it wasn't as safe as Juliana hoped. Robert had only been there a year when the hermitage was burgled. The thieves took everything. All his food supply, his gifts for the poor. The door was battered in and the altar in disarray.

"Robert, I'm so sorry," Juliana said. "Why don't you come and stay up at the house for a while, until we get things fixed?"

But Robert had had enough.

"I can't do this any more. Why is God letting all this happen? I thought I was doing God's will."

"I don't know," said Juliana, gently. "You're still very young..."

"No, I've failed," said Robert. "I'm going to Spofford."

The castle at Spofford belonged to the Percy family, the most powerful clan in the North. If anywhere was safe, it must be Spofford.

"This is the place for me," Robert insisted, through gritted teeth.

But having lived the last few years as a hermit, Robert struggled to adapt to life in town. The smell! And the noise. He could scarcely hear the birds sing. And people just wouldn't leave him alone. They remembered him, you see, from the cave and Saint Hilda's chapel. They expected him to pray for them, and help them, and share the sacraments with them.

I don't do that any more, Robert wanted to say.

But there was something deep in his soul that was meant to be a priest. Something that just wouldn't go away. And Robert had an awful suspicion that he was meant to be a hermit, too.

But... I just can't, he thought.

So, for the second time, he joined a monastery. He ate at set times. He prayed at set times. He slept at set times.

He was bored out of his mind.

Juliana was right, he thought. I was too quick to run away. I wonder if she'll take me back?

He needn't have asked. Juliana was delighted to have Robert on her land once more.

"Now, don't you worry. I'll get everything fixed up properly this time," she said.

She was as good as her word. She sent craftsmen to rebuild the hermitage, with a common hall at its centre, cells for Robert and his companions, and a barn to keep their food stores safe.

This time it was different. Robert had learned from his setbacks, and now worked with four companions. Two of them worked the land, growing barley, kale, leeks and herbs. One helped Robert distribute alms to the poor. And a fourth was Robert's disciple, learning from him the spiritual disciplines of contemplation and prayer. Having someone to teach helped Robert grow in his own spirituality. It was at this time that he received a vision of his departed mother, and was able to pray for her soul. He became at one with the birds and beasts of the land. And he got real pleasure from providing the poor with the meat and fish he no longer indulged in.

Then came the real test.

Juliana was mistress of her own estate, but in Norman society, there was always someone above you. William de Stuteville was Lord of the Forest of Knaresborough. Every estate, church and village in that vast tract of land came under his control. The only man above him was the king. And when he saw Robert's hermitage, daily dealing out charity to the penniless and the vagabonds, the outlaws of the forest, and those who kept their families alive by poaching, he was not happy.

"Tear down those buildings," he commanded. "And have that scum moved on."

"But that's Robert the hermit," one of the men protested. "He's a holy man."

"He's a harbourer of thieves," William growled. "Get rid of him."

The men didn't want to carry out William's orders. One of them dared to remember that the Lord Jesus himself ate with thieves and vagabonds. But when, a few days later, the hermitage was still standing, William was wroth.

"Tear it down! Now!" he roared.

Not a stone was left standing.

What would Robert do? Everything he had worked for, gone again.

"I'm going to have to leave," he told Juliana.

"Oh, Robert! Don't give up again," she said.

Robert gave a grim smile. "I'm moving on, but I'm not giving up. Not this time."

"But where will you go?"

Robert shouldered his pack. "Back to the river."

Back he went with his little community. Back to the caves and the limestone crags. Back to where it had all begun. And ended.

But that no longer worried Robert. An ending – he had come to learn – was a new beginning. Trees let their old leaves fall, so they can be born anew in spring. Geese fly south for the winter, and then north again. Hearts can change, even those as unyielding as a cliff face.

"I'm going to pray for William de Stuteville," he told his friends. "Pray with me."

So they prayed. And just like Anthony of old, Robert found himself wrestling with demons. Robert had discovered the freedom of simple living, but William was shackled by his need to hold onto wealth and power.

"Lord, set him free," Robert prayed.

It wasn't long before a knight came trudging down the treacherous staircase to Robert's cave. It was William. But what a difference in his demeanour! His proud head hung like that of a scolded schoolboy. His feet dragged over the scree.

"Good morning to you, Sir William!" Robert called.

William didn't speak, but knelt meekly on the damp earth.

"Forgive me, Brother Robert," he said. "I have done you a great wrong."

Robert swallowed a smile, and nodded.

William's voice broke. "Pray for me. Please. I am tormented by demons in my sleep. They attack me with pitchforks and fiery maces."

"I've prayed for you already." Robert let the smile break through. He took William's hands. "Those demons are the torments of a guilty conscience. Let them go. I forgive you."

William kissed Robert's hands, as he would have kissed an archbishop's ring. What did rank mean in the kingdom of God?

"I want to make it up to you. I'm giving you all the land hereabouts. No one shall evict you from it. And I'll send you two cows and two horses. And enough food at Christmas to feed thirteen people in need."

"Thank you," said Robert. "It's not necessary, but thank you."

William got stiffly to his feet.

"It's necessary for me," he said.

Things got easier after that, as if Robert had broken through an invisible wall. His brother the mayor came to visit from York, and seeing how Robert now lived, arranged for a small chapel to be built beside Robert's cave. Now there was a centre where people could come to receive alms, the sacrament, and prayer for their ills. Different people lived and worked with Robert over the years, including his last great Soul Friend: Ivo, a Jewish believer in Jesus.

Ivo found hermitage life as tough as Robert once had. At one point, he gave up and ran away. But as he ran, he slipped on a rotten log and fell into a ditch. When he tried to move, his leg wouldn't work. It was broken.

What shall I do now? he thought, through waves of pain.

Just then, Robert's head appeared above the ditch.

"Running away, are we? That's no way to be a disciple."

"Not exactly running now," Ivo grunted.

Robert chuckled. "You should take that as a sign." He paused. "If I pray for your leg to get better, do you promise you won't run off again?"

Ivo caught the humour in his mentor's eye. He grimaced a smile. "Do it."

Robert and Ivo were never parted again. Their finest moment came when Robert was visited by none other than King John, who was staying at Knaresborough Castle. True to form, when the king arrived with his retinue, Robert refused to rise until he had finished his prayers.

"Get up! The king is here," the knights said.

But Robert prayed on.

Then he turned slowly towards the royal party.

"Which one is the king?" he asked.

King John stood a little taller.

Robert held up an ear of corn.

"Has my lord the king the power to make an ear of corn from nothing?"

There was a baffled silence.

Robert shrugged. "In that case, there is no king here but God."

The knights gave a horrified gasp, but Robert was unafraid. His years as a hermit, with all its setbacks, had taught him there is nothing to fear when all is well with your soul.

King John suddenly laughed.

"I like this man! He speaks his mind without fawning and flattery. Not like some."

The knights looked at their feet.

"Tell me Brother Robert, what can I do for you?"

"Nothing, my lord. I lack nothing that I need."

But after the king had gone, Ivo nudged Robert in the ribs.

"You might need nothing, but the people do. The king could grant us food to distribute, and more land to cultivate. It could feed the people for years."

Robert was silent for a moment. Then he sighed. If there was another thing his years had taught him, it was that he wasn't always right.

He turned to Ivo.

"You'd better run along and ask him."

.

Our Lady of Montevergine:

Affirmer of Same Sex Partners

Our Lady of Montevergine:

Affirmer of Same Sex Partners

It was a bitter winter in the mountains when the lovers were discovered. They had tried so hard to keep their secret. But on this day, they could hold back no longer. One hand reached for another. Warm breath whispered against cold cheeks. Lips touched. For one sweet moment, the world fell away.

That was when someone saw.

"They're kissing! Two men. Kissing. Abomination!"

The next moment, chaos.

They had been on their way to worship at the abbey, high on the limestone massif. The hillside was covered in chestnut and beech trees. Once upon a time, Roman eunuchs had worshipped the goddess Cybele there, mourning the death of her lover Attis beneath the pine. Now it was Candlemas - the Celtic feast of Imbolc - when daylight lengthened, and people brought their candles to be blessed, remembering the Presentation of the infant Jesus in the temple. On this day, his mother Mary heard how sorrow would pierce her heart when she saw her son suffer. On this day, worshippers gathered before their own, beloved image of the Madonna, and sang praises to her son.

But all thought of worship had now flown away. Outrage. Disgust. Punishment. These were foremost in the villagers' minds. They seized the lovers, tearing them from one another's arms. Stripped them. Beat them. Dragged them to the woods. There, beneath the bare branches, they tied them to a barren tree and left them to die, as Attis had died in that long-ago myth.

"Food for the wolves. That's what you'll be," their tormentors said.

Night was drawing on fast, and with it temperatures none could survive. A crust of snow covered the ground. The lovers' extremities turned blue. If the wolves didn't hurry, early morning walkers would find two bodies encased in blocks of ice.

But it was not wolves that came.

It was the Madonna.

The Black Madonna, they called her. Our Lady of the Shadow-Side. One who was acquainted with the night and the darkness. Acquainted, too, with prejudice and unjust suffering. Had she not had to watch her son on the cross? That very son who had entrusted to her his beloved, with the words, "He is your son."

The Black Madonna came to her unjustly suffering sons. In the midst of pain, they felt her presence. The clouds parted, and sunshine warmed their faces. The ice began to melt, their bonds to loosen. And a strong but gentle voice seemed to say, "You are beloved."

With a gasp, each of the lovers looked down. His limbs were freed, his life restored.

They fell into each other's arms.

Next year at Candlemas, a procession was heard coming up the mountain. The rumble of ox-carts. The rhythm of tambourines. Singing. Dancing. Flamboyant costumes. The femminielli had come to worship. The sacred, traditional third gender of Naples, whose origins go back to Attis of old. They had come to celebrate and give thanks in the presence of the Black Madonna. "She who gives all and forgives all." For she had rescued the two maligned lovers, and given dignity to minorities.

They still come.

Cædmon:

The Socially Anxious Saint

Cædmon:

The Socially Anxious Saint

assing the Harp is a fine, old tradition. At the end of a feast, to
provide entertainment, each guest must perform a story or song, a
joke or riddle. When the harp comes to you, it's your turn.

In Cædmon's world, everyone knew a story-song. His people were
the Saxons of Northumbria, a Germanic people who had come across
the sea to make their home in Britain. Few of them could read or
write, but that didn't matter. The words sat in their memory. Sagas of
the ancestors, with generations of who begat who. Tales of heroes like
Weyland the Smith or Beowulf. Ancient gods like Woden and Thunor.
Dragons and elves. The tree of the Nine Worlds. Riddles to make you
puzzle or laugh. Wise sayings handed down the generations. All told in
the locked letters of alliteration, in phrases that tripped off the tongue.
All-father. Middle-earth.

Nothing tripped off Cædmon's tongue.

His people were becoming Christians now. King Oswald had
brought monks from Iona under Bishop Aidan, and now there were
monastic missions everywhere. Where Cædmon lived on the North
Yorkshire coast, a whole monastic town had grown up. Forty or fifty
stone cells in two circular enclosures: one for women and one for men.
Refectories, workshops, and a church, of course. And beyond that,
ploughed fields, barns, grazing land and wooden houses. Everyone here
owed their livelihood to Whitby Abbey, and to the powerful lady who
ran it: Mother Hilda.

Now they knew other stories. Judith, who cut off the head of
Holofernes. The Holy Rood, on which the young hero, Christ, defeated
Satan. Mary, choice casket of the Lord, who bore the world a powerful
son. Golden Blossom. All Souls' Helper.

Cædmon remained silent.

It wasn't that he didn't know the tales. He knew them. And he would have liked to sing. But when the community at Whitby gathered for a feast provided by Mother Hilda – whether for a saint's day or the reaping of the oat harvest – the honeyed mead would turn sour in Cædmon's mouth. The chatter was too loud; the smell of other bodies too near. Cædmon would fidget on the bench, scratching at his neck and wrists. He had to get out. He had to get out.

Now the harp was taken down. Soft chords were plucked. A voice, slightly the worse for mead, began chanting, "Weyland among the Wermas suffered woe..." A cheer of recognition. Raucous voices taking up the refrain. The harp was only four people away from Cædmon. A dog bumped against his ankles, seeking bones. Three away. Bile rose to Cædmon's throat. The sea pounded in his ears. Two away. The bench creaked beneath the swaying revellers. He had to get out. Had to get out now.

Cædmon stood beneath the starry sky, hands on knees, gulping cold air. Why did this always happen? No one else seemed troubled. It wouldn't be so bad, he thought, if he had time to compose his song beforehand. But – no – he'd tried that. Whatever words he prepared flew away as soon as the harp came around.

He spat on the ground and stood up. A shiver of cold ran across his shoulders. He would go to the oxen in the byre. It was his turn tonight to keep watch against wolves and raiders. He might as well begin early. Cattle never judged. And there was one less of their number tonight. Dapple had been sacrificed to the feast. The other oxen would miss their friend. Cædmon unlatched the wattled door and went inside.

Here the warmth of bodies was comforting, not claustrophobic. Cædmon went around patting hairy backs and horned heads.

"Good evening, Strongboy. How are you, Clover?" Their breath was the fragrance of hay; even their dung had a sweetness to it. Cædmon shaped some hay into a bed and lay down. A star twinkled between the reed thatching of the roof. His mind drifted to Sunday's sermon, the monk rendering the holy Latin text into English. *In the beginning, God created the heavens and the earth.* The heavens as a roof. Middle-earth for mankind. Cædmon began to dream...

"That's all I've got so far." Cædmon's voice trailed off beneath the reeve's stare.

He hadn't wanted to tell the reeve his song. He'd felt embarrassed, singing it to the boy with the ox-goad. But it had been too incredible. To awaken from sleep, still able to remember the song he'd dreamed. And he'd already sung it to the oxen. He had to tell *someone*.

"That's amazing, Master Cædmon," the boy had gasped. "Like what the monks sing. Only I know the words."

"Well, I don't know any Latin." Cædmon had shrugged. "And the angel told me to sing what I know."

"An angel!" If the boy's eyes had got any wider, they would no longer have fitted in his head. "You have to tell the reeve. Come on!"

The reeve looked straight at Cædmon, solemn in his embroidered hat and tunic. As the village lawman, there was no greater worldly authority.

But Cædmon's tale went beyond things of this earth.

"You say an angel told you to sing?" The reeve's brow creased.

"And I told him I couldn't sing." Cædmon sighed. He'd explained this already. "But he said I had to sing to him. Her. Them." It was beyond Cædmon's knowledge whether angels have genders.

It was beyond the reeve's knowledge, too.

"We must take this song to the Mother Abbess," he said.

Cædmon's throat tightened. Mother Hilda was an ætheling, related to the kings of Northumbria. A holy abbess; a learned scholar. What could he say to such a woman? His words would fly away, as they did on the mead bench.

But the reeve was already leading the way.

And that was how Cædmon came to stand before Hilda and her holy scholars, stuttering and looking at his shoes as he recounted his dream of the angel, and the song of Creation he had been given to sing.

> And *after prepared for men the land,*
> The Almighty Lord.

Cædmon tugged his forelock.

"That's all, my lady."

The scholars were whispering to one another. Between the drum-beats in his ears, Cædmon caught phrases like "doctrinally sound" and "very helpful for the lay folk". He gripped the seams of his sheepskin vest and tried to take slow breaths. At least in the sparse surroundings of Hilda's council chamber, there was no chance of stifling.

"Cædmon, I'd like you to do something for me," Mother Hilda said when the whispering stopped. "Go with Brother Oftor here. He will teach you a new story from sacred scripture. I wish you to learn it and compose a song about it. Can you do that?"

You didn't say no to an ætheling.

"Yes, my lady."

Could he do it again? Turn Holy Scripture into the song of his people. Last time, it had come to him in a dream; this time he would have to do it waking. Yet Mother Hilda believed he now had a gift. And Cædmon felt excited by that. He felt the urge to sing, to make verses. The holy hush of the monastery was unlike the boisterous mead hall. There was space to think. He wasn't expected to versify on the spot. He could take his time, practise, commit it to heart. He could start again if he went wrong; no one would laugh. Who would dream of laughing at a man in the presence of Abbess Hilda?

Cædmon went back to the byre and closed his eyes.

"Excellent. Very good, Cædmon."

He was back in the abbess's council chamber, surrounded by scholars. It helped if he kept his eyes shut to sing, and rocked forward and back on his feet. But he had found another song within him. And he had sung it.

"You are currently a bondsman on our land, working as an ox-herd?"

"Yes, Lady Abbess."

Mother Hilda's eyes were penetrating. But Cædmon thought he caught a twinkle in them at her next words.

"I have a new job for you. How would you like to be a monk?"

"A monk? Me? I'm not... I can't..."

"We are none of us worthy of the task," Mother Hilda said. "Æthelings included. But if you're good enough for an angel, you're good enough for me."

Cædmon shuffled his feet.

"But monks read. I can't read."

"It will come," said Mother Hilda. "And it won't matter at first, for I have a particular task for you. Every week, Brother Oftor will teach you a new passage of scripture. You will turn it into verse. And when you have the verse by heart, you will go to the scriptorium and sing it to the clerks. I wish your songs to be put down in writing. Then they can be circulated to other monastic centres, to teach the young and the unlettered the faith of Our Lord."

Cædmon's eyes widened. Writing! The magic of ink and parchment. Turning breath into visual form. Giving a person's thoughts and words immortality. People might read his song ten years from now. A hundred years? A thousand years?

He looked at Abbess Hilda. She was smiling.

"Yes," he said.

Winefride:

The Headless Healer

Winefride:

The Headless Healer

C an the scene of a crime become a place of healing? Many would recoil from the idea. Yet, time and again, history has shown that it can indeed be so.

Gwenffrewi knew about healing. Her uncle and Soul Friend, the saintly Beuno, had taught her the ways of prayer and herbalism. She had joined him at his little community on the banks of the River Dee in North Wales. Not that everyone approved her choice of vocation, as you will shortly hear.

One day, Gwenffrewi was bathing in the river. Not just a source of cleanliness, Gwenffrewi's people celebrated water as the source of life, which had existed in purity before the creation of the world. Much like the Christ himself, in whose waters Gwenffrewi had been baptised. It was one of the three great healing forces known to her people. Each body of water was a mystical place, a gateway to the Otherworld. A place in which the Salmon of Wisdom might swim, imparting new insights to the seeker.

But if Gwenffrewi was growing in holiness and healing, the opposite was true of her former betrothed. Caradoc, son of Alan. He resented the insult to his dignity struck by Gwenffrewi's choosing a celibate life. Day by day, his lust and jealousy grew within him like a canker, until he could stand it no longer. He would take the maid he had been promised, by fair means or foul.

Unbeknown to Gwenffrewi, Caradoc crouched in the brush while she bathed. And when she emerged, he sprang. A vicious hound pulling down a doe. Gwenffrewi kicked and fought. She screamed, but the spot she had chosen was deliberately remote. Slick with the river, she slithered from Caradoc's clutches, and ran for her life.

Caradoc followed, bellowing insults. "Bitch! Slut! I am your master!"

"I have no master but Christ. And he sees you, Caradoc!"

"I see nothing but trees, mud and water. Will they come to your aid? I think not."

Caradoc ran harder. He was a powerful man, trained for battle. Once, twice, Gwenffrewi evaded him. She had almost reached the doors of the church, crying out for her uncle, when Caradoc struck. He swung his mighty battle-axe, and clove Gwenffrewi's head from her body.

Too late, Beuno and his monks came running. A crimson stream flowed from Gwenffrewi's wound, colouring the stone pavement. Beuno sank to his knees with a howl. He turned his streaming eyes on Caradoc, standing unmoved, his weapon still bloodied.

"May the living God curse you for what you have done this day! May the earth swallow you whole!"

Caradoc made an obscene gesture and strode away.

But a miracle had already taken place. Where Gwenffrewi's head had fallen, a stream had sprung up. Water, pure and healing. Making the moss around it smell of frankincense.

"A holy well," one of the monks breathed.

Beuno tenderly took his niece's severed head and washed it in the water. He thought of the tales of his people: of Bran the Blessed, slain in battle, his severed head kept magically alive on its journey down the Welsh coast. The head was known to be the seat of the soul. What marvels might Gwenffrewi's soul achieve, even in this place of violence?

Beuno stitched the head back onto the body, and laid it out in the church. By morning, the wound between head and body had healed. Gwenffrewi looked just as she had in life.

"A holy, healing well, indeed," Beuno agreed with his monk.

Before he left that place to continue his wandering life, Beuno declared that anyone who sought aid at the spring and dipped three times in its waters would find healing.

The mute witnesses of trees, mud and water that Caradoc had scorned proved his undoing. A year later, in battle on marshy ground, the legs of

Caradoc's horse gave way. He was sucked into the mire, dragged down by the weight of his weapons, and enmeshed by his chainmail. His enemies dealt the killing blow, and Caradoc was ended, swallowed by the earth.

But the miracles at Gwenffrewi's well multiplied. Many and many were the pilgrims who found healing in its waters. Kings and commoners alike. As in the tale of Finn and the Salmon of Wisdom, a wound became a womb, bringing godly things to birth in the place that became known as Trafonic, or Holywell. In English, they called Gwenffrewi by the name of Winefride, and told tales of how she had put on her head and come to life again. Much like the tale told in the Middle Ages of the Green Knight, who met Sir Gawain at Lud's Church, not far to the west of Trafonic. For tales will grow and multiply wherever healing is to be found, and are a source of healing in themselves.

It was not only bodies that were healed at Holywell, but divisions also. Just as Gwenffrewi's severed head and body came together again, so a severed land and church were united at Saint Winefride's Well, though centuries lay between.

Think of the Wars of the Roses, years of civil strife between Yorkists and Lancastrians. When her son beat Richard III to become Henry VII, Margaret Beaufort gave thanks by commissioning the star-shaped well, chapel and shrine still to be seen at Holywell today. And though she had lived in enmity with Elizabeth Woodville and her seed, yet the two mothers let their children be married to form the House of Tudor, thus ending those long wars.

When division came again, in the form of the Reformation, the stones were scattered, images were whitewashed, and inns were closed. But pilgrims never ceased to come, and healings never cease to happen. Elizabeth Roberts recovered from a stroke. Catherine Moore was cured of blindness. On Saint Winefride's Day, 1629, more than a thousand people made a pilgrimage to the well.

Again, there was division, when revolution – bloodless in England alone – set William of Orange against his father-in-law James Stewart. James prayed at Holywell's chapel; William ransacked it. But still the pilgrims came.

And when at last Britain put these divisions behind her, a hospice reopened, with a thousand guests in the first year. Both the Roman

Catholic and Orthodox churches organise pilgrimages to the place known as the Lourdes of Wales. And visitors of all faiths and none bathe in its healing waters.

What might have been remembered as the scene of a crime, steadfastly remains a place of healing. As Gwenffrewi could have told you it would.

Maughold:

The Bandit Saint

Maughold:

The Bandit Saint

In 1158, Somerled was in Ramsey, the port of the Isle of Man.

Now, this Somerled was a mighty lord, with kin ties among the Norse, the Irish and the Scots. He had lately defeated his kinsman in a sea battle, becoming Lord of Man and the Isles, and had come to Ramsey to look over his spoils.

His men and allies were likewise looking for plunder. One chieftain in particular - GilColum, by name - saw that the islanders had cached all their valuables in Saint Maughold's church, and put their cattle in the churchyard, too.

"A fine reward for our labour," GilColum said. "Free food *and* treasure!"

Somerled scowled.

"You sacrilegious swine!" He looked at GilColum as if the man was something he had trodden in. "You'll not catch me stealing from a church." He turned his back. "Do what you will, but don't come crying to me when it all goes bad."

GilColum barked a laugh. All the more for him, if his commander was too yellow for the job. He told his sons and his sworn men to be ready at dawn. They would surprise the church and any who were hiding there.

In the middle of the night, GilColum felt a poke in his ribs. He opened his eyes and squinted into the darkness of his tent. Only, it was less dark than he expected. There was a strange sort of light coming from a person who stood - and this really unsettled GilColum - a few finger-widths above the ground. The person wore bishop's clothes and carried a crozier.

"Who are you?" GilColum's voice was hoarser than he would have liked.

"Who am I, sunshine? I'm your worst nightmare."

"Is this a dream?" GilColum said. That would make sense, what with the floating bishop and all.

"If you like," said the bishop, and prodded him again.

"Stop that!" GilColum rubbed his ribcage. It hurt. "You don't seem much like a bishop," he added.

The bishop took a seat in GilColum's fur-draped camp chair and leaned back, still floating. He kept the crozier pointed in GilColum's direction.

"I wasn't always a bishop." He put one foot up on GilColum's shield. "I used to be a freebooter. A bandit. Proper cut-throat, I was."

"Good for you," GilColum muttered.

"Shut up. I'm telling a story here." The bishop jabbed with the crozier. "You think you're a badass? Me and my lads, we were going to murder Saint Patrick."

He'd been converting some of my men (the bishop said). I mean, the cheek of it! I was the big noise in the district. Maughold the Knife. This was in Ireland, you understand, near the Boyne. I ran those woods; they were my manor. And he thought he could come driving through in his chariot, with his bell-ringing and his psalm-singing and his so-called strong-man. Well...

(Maughold gave a look that said, *really?!*)

It wasn't hard to ambush him. He was just sitting there, meditating. I could have driven a herd of oxen over him; he wouldn't have flinched. But when it came to doing the deed... Well, how can you slit a man's throat who's deep in the spirit world? What if he came back to haunt you? It just...it didn't feel right.

But that just made me madder. Like he'd got under my skin. So we waited till his party was on the move again, and I got one of the lads to lie down and play dead. And when Patrick and his tribe came along, I shouted, "Oi! Cross-worshipper! Why don't you resurrect this one?"

"I don't think so," was all Patrick said, and drove on.

I reckon I could have knifed him then, but I didn't. I went to get my man on his feet again, but he didn't budge. I shoved him with my foot and I tugged him by his arm and he didn't move. I was properly scared then. Because I reckoned, what if this spirit-walking man had put a curse on him? So I ran after that chariot and I threw myself on my knees, and I begged Patrick to pray to his God. "I should never have mocked you," I said. "I don't know what's happening here, but I want it to stop."

And you know what Patrick said? He said, "You know when the chickens are pecking around in the yard? There's always one that's cock of the walk."

And I nodded because that was me. Cock of the walk. Cock of the Boyne.

"Well, in the spiritual world, Jesus is cock of the walk," he said.

And he prayed for my man, and my man got up. He got up and was right as rain. And I said, "You'd better tell me about this Jesus. Because I need to know."

"That was the start of it," Bishop Maughold said. "I got baptised, renounced the world, and came here to the Isle of Man to do penance on the hills. Hard penance. Lots of fasting." He looked at GilColum. "Even Brigid was impressed by my austerity. Mind you, she was one for multiplying butter and beer. Still. It felt like chains hung around me, when I thought of my past. It was years before I felt really free."

He stood up from the chair and stretched his back. "And the rest is history. Became bishop. Baptised people. Gave my name to the church. You know, the one with the coins and the cattle?"

"So you're *Saint* Maughold?" GilColum gave a look that said, *really?!*

"Yes, I am. And I've got three lessons for you, sunshine. One: Jesus is cock of the walk. Two: even a bandit can be a saint. And three..." He jabbed the crozier hard in GilColum's ribs. "Stay away from my church!"

They say that, when GilColum's men woke the next morning, they found him wide-eyed and gasping for breath, jabbering about a bandit bishop who poked him with a crozier. They decided to leave the church alone, which was probably a wise move.

When Somerled heard of it, it put the fear of God into him. He hoisted anchor and set sail for one of his other islands. Later in life – whether because of this incident or not – he tried to persuade Irish monks to return to Columba's monastery on Iona, which had long since been looted by Viking raiders.

But they never did.

Brendan:

The Respecter of First Nations

Brendan:

The Respecter of First Nations

I t had been a long voyage. A dangerous voyage in uncharted water. They had encountered sea monsters, sirens, burning birds, and thirsting souls. Until they finally reached the Land of Promise.

And now they were leaving.

"I don't understand," said one of the monks. "Aren't we meant to preach the word, build a church, found a community?"

Brother Brendan stopped loading the curragh for a moment, and sat down on a cask. He was the leader of the voyage. It was his vision that had inspired them to leave the Irish shore, and sail among icebergs and volcanic islands, to come to a place nobody knew. From the looks on the monks' faces, they were all keen to know why they were going home so soon.

"Remember when we first heard about this land from Brother Barinthius? A land to the far west, across the ocean. An earthly paradise, abundant in fruit and jewels."

The monks all nodded. "And he was right," one said. "It's just like that."

"And remember when we first came to the great river, and that handsome young man came to greet us?"

Smiles went round the group. The young man in question was a chieftain among his people, and a great friend to the monks. He had spoken peace to them, shared with them the fruits of the land, and given them rich gifts. They knew that he and Brendan had shared many conversations together, speaking of deep matters.

"But will he not grant us land for a monastery, as chieftains have done at home?" someone dared to ask.

Brendan's gaze turned inward. "No. There is no need. He bids us depart, and I agree with his wisdom."

"But why?" the first monk asked again.

"For two reasons." Brendan leaned forward, elbows on his knees. "For one, the Spirit of Christ is already in these people. I see it in our friend as clearly as if the light of the sun shone from his face."

"I think I do, too," said a monk.

"Me too."

"I think I recognise Christ in their teachings," someone said.

"Exactly." Brendan's eyes sparkled. "They seek after the Spirit. They listen to the earth. They revere the hallowed circle, just as we do."

"Like when we pray circling prayers," someone suggested. "And when we draw a circle around the arms of the cross."

"That's right," said Brendan. "What could we teach our hosts that they don't already know? They have already acted like Christ towards us."

"What's the second reason?" said a younger monk.

Brendan grew serious. "Our friend tells us that he foresees a day when this land will become known to the people of our homelands. It will be a day of tribulation. Ships will arrive on these shores as large as floating islands, with masts like a forest of trees. And neither their merchants nor their missionaries will come in humility. They will ravage this land and its people in their lust for gain. They will bring others here in forced labour and treat them as livestock. They will impose their ways on those who do not wish for it. We must not be like that."

"So that's it then?" said the first monk.

Brendan got to his feet. His knees creaked a little, for he was no longer young.

"That's it. We go home, and we take our stories with us. It's important that people hear about this voyage." He patted the curragh's caulking.

"Let's set sail."

Select Story Sources & Further Reading

Adair, John, *The Pilgrims' Way: Shrines and Saints in Britain and Ireland*. Hampshire: Thames & Hudson, 1978.

Baring-Gould, Sabine, *The Vicar of Morwenstow: A Life of Robert Stephen Hawker, M.A.* London & New York: King/T. Whittaker, 1876. Digitalised by Project Canterbury. <anglicanhistory.org>

Barton, Allan, "St. Melangell – the life and shrine of a 7th century Welsh saint in early Christian Britain", *Antiquarians Anonymous*, YouTube, 26 May 2022.

Briggs, Katharine M., *A Dictionary of British Folk-Tales (Part B)*. London & New York: Routledge, 1991.

Butler, Rev. Allan, *The Lives of the Saints Volume IV: April*. 1866.

Cherry, Kittredge, ed., "Calendar of LGBTQ Saints and Holidays", *Q Spirit*, 2023. <qspirit.net>

Gill, Elaine & Everett, David, *Celtic Pilgrimages*. London: Blandford, 1997.

Healy, Most Rev. Dr., *The Life and Writings of St Patrick*. Dublin: 1905.

Jeff, Amy, *Storyland: A New Mythology of Britain*. London: Riverrun, 2021.

Jongen, Ludo, "St Oda of Brabant, The Blind Princess of Scotland", *Heiligenlevens in Nederland en Vlaanderen*. Amsterdam, 1998. Translation in *Orthodox Christianity*. 12 November 2014. <orthodoxchristian.com>

Kennedy, Patrick, *Legendary Fictions of the Irish Celts*. London: Macmillan, 1866.

"Marcella", *Omnium Sanctorum Hiberniae*, 2012–2023. <omniumsanctorumhiberniae.com>

Massingham, H.J., *Out of Doors Vol. 13*. 10 January 1952. <robertstephenhawker.co.uk>

Moore, A.W., *The Folk-Lore of the Isle of Man*. 1891. <sacred-texts.com>

O'Donavan, J, ed. and trans., *Annals of the Kingdom of Ireland by the Four Masters Vol. 1*. Dublin: 1856. <archive.org>

O'Donoghue, Denis, trans., *Navigatio sancti Brendan abbatio*. 1893.

O'Grady, Standish Hayes, *Silva Gadelica Vol. II* (from *The Book of the Dun Cow*), 1892. Reprint, New York: C Lemma Publishing Corp., 1970. <web.archive.org>

Olsen, Ted, *Christianity and the Celts*. Oxford: Lion Publishing, 2003.

Paintner, Christine Valters, "Feast of St. Gobnait: Go Seek the Place of Your Resurrection", Patheos, 11 Feb 2016. <patheos.com>

Parkinson, Rev. Thomas, *Yorkshire Legends and Traditions*. London: Eliot Stock, 1888.

Sellar, A.M., trans., Saint the Venerable Bede, *Bede's Ecclesiastical History of England*. London: George Bell & Sons, 1907.

Sellner, Edward C., *Wisdom of the Celtic Saints*. Notre Dame, IL: Ave Maria Press, 1993.

Simpson, Ray, *Great Celtic Christians*. Stowmarket: Kevin Mayhew Ltd, 2004.

Simpson, Ray, *Saints of the Isles*. Stowmarket: Kevin Mayhew Ltd, 2003.

St. Hubert Club of Great Britain, The, "Who was St. Hubert?", 2022. <sainthubertclub.org.uk>

Tsames, Demetrios G., *Materikon (Lives of the Holy Mothers) Vol. 1*. Thessalonica: Ekdoseis, 1990.

Weichberger, Lilly & McIntosh, Kenneth, *Brigid's Mantle: A Celtic Dialogue Between Pagan and Christian*. Vestal, NY: Anamchara Books, 2015.

Acknowledgements

This book would not have happened without the help and support of many people. Thanks especially to the EDI silent prayer group in the Community of Aidan & Hilda - a silent Zoom might sound crazy to outsiders, but it's a highlight of my week! Thanks to my siblings at Open Table Bradford and Clayton Baptist Church. To my local community of Clayton village. And of course to my actual family, especially Mum and Mick.

Thanks again to Anna for her beautiful illustrations - you have outdone yourself this time!

Thanks again to Helen Hart and the team at SilverWood Books for creating the book you now hold in your hand.

To the Centre for Folklore, Myth & Magic at Todmorden, Scargill House, and The Order of the Holy Paraclete at Whitby for the use of your libraries. To every online library project that makes it possible to read things like *The Book of the Dun Cow* without traipsing physically around the country - as a chronic pain/fatigue sufferer, I can't tell you how helpful that is!

To you, the reader, without whom this would all be pointless.

To all the cats, especially my best friend Ember, and dear, departed Nutmeg and Mr Tumble.

And to the saints and storytellers of the past, who inspired this book, and continue to inspire me and help me through the dark days. In the words of Julian of Norwich, "All shall be well, and all shall be well, and all manner of things shall be well."

Supporters

This book has been crowdfunded by Kickstarter. Many thanks to our generous supporters listed below, and those who choose to remain anonymous.

Lucy
Anon
Kayden Harper
Rkh260
Gemma
Dagmar Baumann
Mars Core
Kiosmic
Georgina
Sarah Williams
Suzanne Allsop
Ron Roehl
Penny Warren
Serpentmoon
The Selkie Delegation
Craig Esser
MorpheusSleeps
Hannah Hazlehurst
Kay Black
Paul & Laura Trinies
C Rosser
Vicki Hsu
Becky Farrell
Drew G Jackson
Colleen Feeney
Sophia Hurd
Camilla Ballinger

Megan Krantz
Rebekah
Lynden Wade
Benjamin Welles
Kerenza
H Baxter
Anonymous
Douglas Cumming
Lisa Quigley
Em Kenny
Kneeky Turner
Maddy
Simon Reed
Patricia Ramsey
Mark Greenall
     (Purple Triangle)
Amelia Ace Armande
Erika Sanderson
Sean
I Carolyn Shaw
Viannah E Duncan
Jenny S
L Penny
Anna Henseleit
AslansCompass
Debra Lovelace
Ruth Parkinson

Penny Blackburn
Claire
Ray
Sam
Mel
Marva
Daniel